I0720404

His Majesty's Hounds – Book 4

Sweet and Clean Regency Romance

Being Lady Harriet's Hero

Arietta Richmond

Dreamstone Publishing © 2017

www.dreamstonepublishing.com

Copyright © 2017 Dreamstone Publishing and Arietta Richmond

ISBN: 1925499197

ISBN-13: 978-1-925499-19-3

Books by Arietta Richmond

His Majesty's Hounds

Claiming the Heart of a Duke

Intriguing the Viscount

Giving a Heart of Lace (a prequel to Winning the Merchant Earl)

Being Lady Harriet's Hero

Enchanting the Duke (coming soon)

Redeeming the Marquess (coming soon)

Healing Lord Barton (coming soon)

Winning the Merchant Earl (coming soon)

Loving the Bitter Baron (coming soon)

Rescuing the Countess (coming soon)

Attracting the Spymaster (coming soon)

The Derbyshire Set

A Gift of Love (Prequel short story)

A Devil's Bargain (Prequel short story - coming soon)

The Earl's Unexpected Bride

The Captain's Compromised Heiress

The Viscount's Unsuitable Affair

The Count's Impetuous Seduction

The Rake's Unlikely Redemption

The Marquess' Scandalous Mistress

A Remembered Face (Bonus short story – coming soon)

The Marchioness' Second Chance (coming soon)

A Viscount's Reluctant Passion (coming soon)

Lady Theodora's Christmas Wish

The Duke's Improper Love (coming soon)

Other Books

The Scottish Governess (coming soon)

The Earl's Reluctant Fiancée (coming soon)

The Crew of the Seadragon's Soul Series, (coming soon - a set of 10 linked novels)

ARIETTA RICHMOND

Dedication

For everyone who had the grace to be patient while this book, and every other book that I have written, was coming into existence, who provided cups of tea, and food, when the writing would not let me go, and endured countless times being asked for opinions.

For the readers who inspire me to continue writing, by buying my books! Especially for those of you who have taken the time to email me, or to leave reviews, and tell me what you love about these books, and what you'd like to see more of – thank you – I'm listening, I promise to write more about your favourite characters.

For my growing team of beta readers and advance reviewers – it's thanks to you that others can enjoy these books in the best presentation possible!

And for all the writers of Regency Historical Romance, whose books I read, who inspired me to write in this fascinating period.

vi

Chapter One

Lord Geoffrey Clarence tapped on the rickety door before opening it carefully. No matter how many times he had been here, the whole place still felt fragile to him – he was a big man, and worried that, if he pushed too hard, the stairs or the doorframe would simply break.

On the other side of the door, the room was warm as the early winter afternoon's sunlight streamed in through the large glass windows. Cecil Carlisle, Baron Setford, waved him to a chair and handed him a cup of coffee, which was, as usual, perfectly prepared, and exactly as he liked it. One day, Geoffrey thought, he would find out how Setford managed that – the miraculous appearance of perfect hot coffee, when there seemed no-one else in evidence, and there had been no exact time for the meeting.

For now, he simply accepted the cup, and sipped with pleasure. This was a place in which he could be totally relaxed, certain that there was no danger – which was a sensation to treasure.

"You've done well these last few months, m'boy. The Prince Regent appreciates still being alive."

Geoffrey raised an eyebrow, a somewhat cynical expression on his face.

"Is that 'appreciates' in a 'here's your reward' way, or in a 'since you're so clever at this, here's your next nasty job' way?"

Setford guffawed and leant back in his chair, his piercing pale grey eyes sparkling. Once the laughter had run its course, his face took on a more serious expression.

"You always were damn sharp – straight to the crux of it. And you're right about it being able to go either way. But in this case, it's actually a bit of both. There's a reward, but there's also another 'nasty job' as you so aptly put it."

He reached over to the table beside him, and produced a folder. From the folder, he withdrew a large sealed document. Sealed with the Prince Regent's seal, if Geoffrey wasn't mistaken. Silently, Setford passed it to Geoffrey.

"That's the reward."

Geoffrey broke the seal carefully. A minute's perusal of the document revealed that he was now the owner of a rather large estate, located not too far from Charlton's country seat, Pendholm Hall. An estate called, apparently, Witherwood Chase. He wondered what it was like. Gifts from Prinny had an alarming potential to come with 'issues'. Who knew if the estate had been well maintained or not? He may have just been gifted an expensive repair and maintenance bill.

"Do you know anything about it?"

Setford shook his head.

"Nothing at all, beyond the fact that it has reverted to the crown after the previous owner proved treasonous. So you may find interesting things within its walls. And that's the 'nasty job' bit. We are not at all sure that we have all of the conspirators in the treason. So, you need to develop a sudden desire to look into your new property – in VERY great detail. I would personally be extremely grateful if you manage to find the papers and other evidence that we believe are hidden there."

Geoffrey grimaced – digging through dusty cellars and trying to find secret compartments in wainscoting might have amused him when he was a boy, but it certainly wasn't exactly appealing now! Still, a decent estate wasn't a gift one received every day. It might even turn out to be a pleasant place. With Charlton's family nearby, he'd even have good company if he wanted it.

And... far better to spend the next few months, and then the holiday season, in a place of his own, rather than in his miserable brother's house, watching him bicker with his miserable wife. Alfred's opinion of what Geoffrey should do with his life stopped at 'being a good heir and doing everything the way I do'.

Setford watched him carefully, and smiled wryly as the expressions flowed across Geoffrey's face.

"Yes, I rather thought you'd appreciate having a bolt hole of your own, and a damn good reason to stay there."

"Astute as ever, sir. I just hope it's not quite a crumbling ruin – this 'reward' doesn't happen to come with any convenient cash, to help deal with any repairs needed, does it?"

Setford laughed again.

"A gift from Prinny, that came with money?? Surely you know better!"

Geoffrey sighed, and went back to the excellent coffee.

~~~~~

Five sennights later.

Lady Harriet Edgeworth arrived in the morning room at Pendholm Hall like a whirlwind (which was not an uncommon occurrence...). Her brother looked up with an amused smile on his face. Charlton Edgeworth, Viscount Pendholm, was quite used to his sister's tendency to be all energy – behaving like a good little society miss was challenging for her at the best of times, and here at Pendholm Hall, where they had grown up, she simply didn't try most of the time.

The two dogs lying by the hearth looked up, their sleep disturbed by her arrival, but, after a few thumps of their tails, they settled back to rest.

"Did you have a good ride Harriet?"

"Wonderful! Thank you again for buying Moonbeam for me – she is just the best horse that I have ever had! Poor John can barely keep up with me, and Miss Carpenter quite refuses to ride with me anymore."
~~~~~

Charlton knew that the last statement was the most important to Harriet. His sister's long-suffering companion had never been much of a rider, and Harriet had been making her life miserable by causing her to ride as often as possible during the last year.

"Where did you ride to today?" Lady Pendholm asked her daughter, smiling at her exuberance.

Harriet's face took on an expression which could be described as 'false innocence', if one was to be uncharitable.

"Oh, just across the park to the river near Witherwood Chase." Whilst her tone of voice was casual, the whole effect was spoilt by the blush that coloured Harriet's cheeks. Her mother's eyes sparkled with a mischief that made it quite obvious where Harriet's volatile demeanour came from.

"It's a lovely ride, isn't it? You didn't, perchance, happen to see Lord Geoffrey did you? I wanted to invite him to dinner tomorrow."

Harriet's blush deepened, to a colour that was not exactly flattering against her dark gold hair. Her family teased her about her interest in Lord Geoffrey. They were sure that she would grow out of it. She was equally sure that she would not. It was not a childish infatuation, not at all.

She had decided, when she had first met him, just after he had heroically saved her brother and mother's lives, as well as the lives of four other people, that he was wonderful. He looked like the hero he was.

And he was going to be her hero. No matter how long it took for her to convince him.

Whilst she had been the toast of the Season earlier in the year, and had been flattered by the attention of a large number of eligible gentlemen, she had not wanted to marry any of them. She had shuddered at the thought. She knew what she wanted, and she planned to get it.

"He did ride by, in the distance. Unfortunately he didn't see me." She sighed in disappointment, firmly telling herself that he had NOT ignored her, that he simply hadn't seen her. "So you'll have to send a footman over with a message to invite him."

Watching Harriet's eyes light up at the thought of Lord Geoffrey coming to dinner, her mother had a hard time not laughing. But it really wouldn't do to belittle her daughter's *tendre* for the man – that would, of a certainty, only make her more stubborn.

"I will do so this morning."

Harriet produced a large smile at her mother's words, and whirled out of the room again, to change from her riding habit to a gown suitable for luncheon.

Chapter Two

Lord Geoffrey's first sight of Witherwood Chase had not been inspiring. The gates were uneven and looked not to have been shut for a very long time, the drive was rutted so badly that he feared for the wheels of his carriage, and the winter bare trees that lined it did nothing to improve the prospect.

The house itself was larger than he might have expected – a graceful and well-proportioned H shape, where the side wings enclosed a formal garden and a grand approach to the porticoed entry at the front. Between the wings at the rear was a terrace onto a once elegant herb and scent garden, which was protected from the elements by a decorative wall between the ends of the wings. An impressive four stories of windows had looked down on him as he alighted from his carriage and approached the doors.

Everything had shown signs of some recent neglect, but not so much as he had feared might be the case. He had discovered, upon his arrival, that the property had come with staff – a point which had not been mentioned in the missive granting him ownership.

The staff (a butler of a rather venerable age, a housekeeper, an estate manager, two footmen, a cook, two maids and two grooms, plus a gardener) had responded to his arrival with courtesy, but obvious suspicion. Now, a month later, as Christmas approached, that had at least faded to them treating him with cordial distance. That suspicion and distance was not aiding his investigations one bit.

He had added another two footmen, and a valet, to his staff – men who came well recommended, via Baron Setford, and who had skills and knowledge not commonly found in footmen or valets – which they took great care not to reveal to the other staff. The house had also seen a continuing parade of persons in the business of providing various types of repairs, cleaning services, furniture supply and restoration, and more. The costs were rather alarming, but the ledgers presented by the estate manager had at least given him hope that the place might actually be capable of funding itself, with a little attention to the tenant farmers.

That realisation had led to a round of visits to the village, and all of the tenant's cottages, to assess what repairs would be needed, and to start the long process of building their trust. It was increasingly obvious that the previous owner, apart from having been foolish enough to commit treason, had never been a very likeable man, and had never put the slightest effort into caring about those whose work generated much of his income. Geoffrey hoped that, eventually, the tenants would trust him enough to actually reveal exactly what they had so disliked about the previous master of Witherwood Chase.

On this particular day, Geoffrey had just returned from checking on the repairs to various farmers' cottages. He was well pleased with progress, as the fact that their cottages had been restored to a weatherproof state, before the worst of winter, had led to a markedly more positive attitude from the farmers and their families.

The day was brisk, and the early snow had partly melted in the weak sunlight. He had enjoyed being out and moving, as he always did. At one point, in the distance near the small river that bounded one side of his land, he had seen Lady Harriet riding that quality grey mare that Charlton had bought her a few months ago. He had admired her seat, and, if he was honest, her fine figure, from a distance, but had carefully pretended not to notice her. However attractive the chit was, she was only eighteen, and the sister of one of his closest friends – definitely not a girl that he should be getting interested in!

Handing Rajah to the waiting groom and leaving the horse to his well-earned rub down, Geoffrey took himself inside, via the kitchen door – why walk all the way around the house in the cold and the sleet which had begun to fall? Cook gave him her best disapproving look, glaring at the small trail of wet slush left on the floor from his boots. He swept her a somewhat mocking bow.

"I must apologise, Mrs Chester, for trailing mud in here. But I quite refuse to freeze for any longer than necessary. I am certain that the maid can manage to deal with it expeditiously."

Her expression suggested that his frivolous attitude was unsuitable for a Lord, but she said nothing of it, simply turning back to the preparation of what looked like a sumptuous meal.

As he stepped into the hall, on his way to his study to warm up with a glass of good brandy in front of the fire, his butler intercepted him.

"Good afternoon, my Lord. A letter has just been delivered for you." Barnstable proffered the letter on an aged and elegant silver salver.

"Thank you, Barnstable." Geoffrey swept the letter up as he continued towards the study, determinedly ignoring Barnstable's rather pointed look at the final drips of muddy snow which had fallen from his boots onto the patterned marble floor. This having a collection of staff was still a strange experience. So many years of looking after himself during the war had made him unused to needing others, or paying any heed to their fussiness.

Still, there were some advantages – such as the excellent meals that Mrs Chester produced each day. Brandy in hand, he dropped into his favourite chair with a sigh, and brought his attention to the letter. It was addressed simply 'Lord Geoffrey' in a hand which he recognised. He wondered what Lady Sylvia wished of him.

Opening it, he smiled. It was, for a letter from a member of the *ton*, utterly short and to the point. It invited him to dine with Lady Sylvia and her family, at Pendholm Hall, the following day. A relaxing, and likely entertaining, evening in Charlton's company was definitely appealing.

Lady Sylvia was also an excellent conversationalist, and a pleasure to speak with, as she was intelligent, and not afraid to have opinions. The only thing which gave him a moment's pause was knowing that it would also be an evening spent in Lady Harriet's company.

Since the unfortunate incidents of early in the year, when he had been forced to dispose of some ruffians to save the lives of a number of people, including Charlton and his mother, Lady Harriet had conceived a vision of him as some sort of hero. Which idea rather horrified him. He was certain that she harboured a *tendre* for him, and he found dealing with her somewhat obvious regard difficult. Especially as the girl was so damned attractive!

So be it. He would not let the chit's obsession with making him out as a 'hero' stop him from spending time with Charlton. Charlton Edgeworth, Viscount Pendholm, was, like Lord Geoffrey, one of a group of six men who had, during their service in France and Spain, come to be called 'His Majesty's Hounds' for their tenacious ability to sniff out French spies and troop movements, and deal with them. For all of those years, they had been closer than family – each owed the others his life, multiple times over. Geoffrey was overwhelmingly glad that Witherwood Chase was so close to Pendholm Hall.

Leaving his brandy on the side table, he went to his desk and quickly dashed off a reply, accepting the invitation with pleasure. Once his note of acceptance was sanded and sealed, he rang for Barnstable and settled back into his chair. The door opened rapidly and Barnstable came into the room at a rate that belied his appearance of great age.

"Yes, My Lord?"

"Please have Peterson deliver this letter to Pendholm Hall immediately."

Barnstable took the letter, bowed, and left the room.

Staring into the flames, and sipping his brandy, Lord Geoffrey contemplated his progress with his mission. Digging into the secrets of the house had become more of a pleasure for him than he had expected. For, as he did, he discovered fascinating things about the building, and he was, as well, making it his own. He had not quite realised, until he came to Witherwood Chase, how soul destroying it had been to live in his brother's house, dependent upon him. The gift of Witherwood Chase may have come with a mission which was frustrating and slow, but it had been a gift without price as far as its impact on his state of mind.

He was beginning to realise just how deeply blue-devilled he had become after his return from war. Working for Setford had begun to turn that around, but the simple fact of having his own place had been the biggest factor in shifting his view of the world. He still had days when it all seemed pointless (usually after digging through yet another few rooms of the house, and finding nothing more thrilling than mouse droppings and tasteless paintings), but they were less now.

He was, however, beginning to be annoyed. Setford was so certain that there was something here to find, yet he had been singularly unsuccessful, to date, in finding any trace of either papers, or possible hiding places. But, he reminded himself, he had barely begun.

He had searched, in detail, barely more than a quarter of the house so far – he could not expect this to be easy, or Setford's men would have found everything when the treasonous previous owner was captured. The house was old – at least 500 years old - and had been extended many times. There was a warren of cellars and a tangle of tiny attic rooms, as well as the large quantity of rooms on the main floors. Add to that all of the outbuildings, and the scope for potential hiding places was extensive.

He had the feeling that some of the staff knew more about the house, and the events here before the conspirators had been caught, than they were telling him – he would simply have to find a way to get them to talk of it. He wondered, not for the first time, if the house had hidden passages and rooms. It was old enough to have been here at a time when hidden rooms, priest holes or secret passages and tunnels might have been needed, to escape the ravages of civil war. But if those things were there, he had yet to see any sign of them.

Perhaps, tomorrow, he would take a different approach. Leaving the rooms in the main part of the house for later, he would start with the attics, and see what interesting things he found there, then work his way from there down, a floor at a time, until he reached the deepest cellars. Attics in houses this old often contained items stored generations ago, so, if nothing else, he might actually have fun discovering items from bygone eras. And, should they include further truly ugly paintings, at least he could sell the damn things, to recoup some of the costs of putting the place back in order!

Having a plan made him feel more cheerful about it all.

Leaning back, he eyed the faded tapestry on the wall in front of him and sighed – another thing needing cleaning and care. Now that the drapes on the windows to the side of it had been replaced, the sad state of the tapestry was very obvious. Oh well, it could wait for now. Right now, as he sipped the last of his brandy, food was the most pressing thing on his mind.

Barnstable, as if he had heard the thought, chose that moment to appear at the door, announcing that dinner was served in the dining room. Lord Geoffrey rose and followed him from the room.

Chapter Three

The following day Lord Geoffrey took himself up to the attics, much to Barnstable's horror.

"My Lord! The attics are full of… um… a… rather historic… collection of… things… Not to mention dust, dirt, and probably rodents! Surely a gentleman like yourself doesn't wish to dig about in all that!"

"Oh, what fustian, Barnstable, stop fussing. I will, eventually, stick my nose into every nook and cranny this rather curious construction of a house has to offer. A little dust and dirt never hurt anyone. I might even find something of value – at least I can hope. If nothing else, I can ascertain whether the roof is leaking anywhere!"

Barnstable managed to look both offended and dignified at once (rather an achievement, Geoffrey thought) and, bowing stiffly, took himself out of the room. Geoffrey followed. As he entered the hallway, he saw one of the footmen moving hurriedly in the direction of the servant's stairs. Idly, he wondered what the rush was.

Putting that from his mind, he made his way up a rather impressive number of stairs, finally arriving at the door into the attics. It was a rather small door, and Lord Geoffrey, being a rather large man, squeezed through it carefully. He noted, with amusement, that Barnstable was right – he had already acquired smears of dust and dirt on his clothing – and that by just going through the door.

The attics proved to be a warren of rooms, spread across the under roof space of all of the main part of the house and the wings, sometimes in multiple levels, with small flights of stairs between them. To start with, all he did was wander from room to room, trying to get a feel for the scale of it. He found a section with a large rainwater cistern – no doubt responsible for the luxury of running water which was present in parts of the house, and a multitude of rooms full of stored furniture, paintings, and God knows what else, all covered in dust sheets.

Mid-afternoon, just as he was contemplating returning downstairs in search of luncheon, Lord Geoffrey opened another door. All thought of food left him instantly. This room, unlike the others, was ordered. Its walls were covered in carefully structured racks, stands and display cases were placed neatly about the space, and, on every rack, in every case, on every stand, were weapons and armour.

This one room was a museum collection of weaponry from centuries past and times recent. It was, in one room, more weapons that Geoffrey had ever seen before – including the armoury tent in their field camps during the war!

For a man whose distinguishing ability was consummate skill with weapons, this was the ultimate find. He felt rather like a small child presented with a room full of toys.

The swords, in particular, called to him. The light of his lantern reached into shadowy corners, drawing sparkling glints from sharpened metal. Even through the light layer of dust, he could see that they had been well cared for – as if someone, until very recently, had come here often, dusted, polished and oiled everything, to keep it in the best of condition. He wondered who. It did not matter.

The next few hours disappeared into a haze of delighted exploration, as he opened cases, lifted weapons down from the wall, and generally did an inventory of the contents of the room. This was certainly not what Setford wanted him to find, but, for himself, this alone was reward enough for all of the tedious time he had spent, and would spend, searching for the blasted treasonous papers.

"My Lord! My Lord?? Where are you?" Barnstable's voice came to him, distantly echoing through the attic rooms.

"Here Barnstable – in the north-west wing, I think."

Footsteps approached after a few minutes, and Barnstable peered through the door.

"Oh my!"

Barnstable's shock was obviously not feigned, as he stared in some awe at the contents of the room.

"I gather that you were not aware of this collection?"

"No, my Lord, not at all. It is... impressive, isn't It?"

"Quite. Even if I find nothing else of interest in the entire house, this is worth any amount of dust dirt and poking about. Now, what was it you came to tell me?"

"My Lord, it is nearly five – I believe that you are due at Pendholm Hall at seven, for dinner?"

"Is it? I quite lost track of time up here, with no light but my lantern. I'd best hurry then. Thank you."

Lord Geoffrey turned, and, with a last longing look at the beautiful collection of weaponry, closed the door and followed Barnstable out of the attics.

~~~~~

Lady Harriet was fidgeting. She had tried to read, and found herself unable to concentrate, even on the new novel that had just arrived. She had considered embroidery, and instantly discarded the notion – she did not do it well at the best of times. So now, she was wandering about the family parlour, randomly picking up the various small statues and items on the mantle and shelves, fiddling with them a few moments, then replacing them, just to keep herself busy. For sitting still was an impossibility, when, at any moment, Lord Geoffrey might arrive.

Had they been in the morning room, she might have sat at the pianoforte, and allowed herself to release her tensions into the music. That always worked. But, alas, this room did not contain an instrument, so she was left to fidgeting beneath her mother's amused and tolerant gaze.
~~~~~

Lady Sylvia observed her daughter with interest. Harriet had, it seemed, put more effort into her appearance this evening than usual, even allowing for the fact that they were expecting a guest. That would be because of who the guest was, she surmised. She was still quite uncertain about Harriet's obsession with Lord Geoffrey – he seemed to be of a temperament rather more quiet than Harriet's bright volatility. Perhaps that was part of why he appealed to her? But, for a man like that, would Harriet seem appealing, or merely childishly annoying?

For now, given that Lord Geoffrey's behaviour had always been utterly correct and polite, and that he was a man to whom she owed her life, as well as being one of Charlton's closest friends, she was willing to simply let things proceed as they would. Her thoughts were interrupted by the sound of the front door knocker, followed by the measured tread of the butler's feet on the marble foyer floor.

At those sounds, Harriet froze, arrested in mid motion as her hand reached for yet another trinket, and she stood a moment, a flush rising to her cheeks, and her heart beating hard, as she composed herself, ready to greet Lord Geoffrey when he was shown into the room. Then, with a deep breath, she moved again – turning to face the door just as it opened.

Lord Geoffrey was, as always, immaculately presented. The dark blue superfine of his perfectly cut coat displayed his powerful shoulders in a manner that quite stole Harriet's breath. It was ever so – no matter how much she prepared herself for his presence, each time the impact was just as great. Her breath stalled, her heart beat harder, and her ability to think became alarmingly dimmed.

He advanced into the room, bowing over her mother's hand, then hers. Somehow, she stammered a greeting in response to his. He turned to greet her brother. Her eyes drank him in as he spoke with Charlton, who was laughing at some comment Lord Geoffrey had made.

They all settled into the comfortable seats around the fireplace, and conversation flowed freely. As the initial effects of his presence wore off, Harriet regained her ability to think, and found that she had missed, apparently, quite a bit of conversation – it seemed that Charlton and Lord Geoffrey were discussing the events of the last year.

"It seems so surreal to me, Charlton, that it is, this week, a year since we returned from the war. So much has changed! Then, we were exhausted, heartsick from years of war, and unsure of how to go about life again, here. Now, we are all so much more settled, Hunter is married, you will be married in little more than a month, Raphael is off travelling and actually enjoying life, Gerry has been given a title – deservedly so – and Bart thinks he's found the perfect place to breed his horses. And as for me – I am finding that Witherwood Chase is far more interesting than I had expected. Having a place of my own has its challenges, but it is infinitely better than living on Alfred's sufferance."

Lord Geoffrey's rich, deep voice flowed over her, and she had to agree with his sentiments – it had been a remarkable year. It seemed that Charlton also agreed.

"Indeed, Geoff, it is hard to believe that Christmas is almost upon us. I will be glad to see the others at Meltonbrook Chase for twelfth night, although it seems that Raphael will not return in time – he will be sorely missed!"

"I have to assume that there is some great profit to be had from this venture, for it to have dragged him away for so long. We will simply have to wait to find out though – he's been remarkably close about it all. It's bad timing from my point of view – being purely selfish – Witherwood Chase, it turns out, is full of a great hoard of things that have been shoved away in its attics, rooms and cellars forever – perhaps centuries! Including the largest collection of ugly paintings that I have ever seen. I will be selling them, with Raphael's help, I hope. With a bit of luck, our canny merchant can help me actually make the place pay for all of the repairs I've done since I got here!"

"The previous occupant had bad taste then?" Lady Sylvia's voice was amused. "I never met the man, even though we were close neighbours. He never seemed to be here when we were. The villagers did sometimes remark on the state of his tenant's cottages though – it seems that he was not a good manager at all, and certainly not popular with his tenants, or anyone else in the district."

"That is very much true my Lady, this month has been one long tale of woe as far as the condition of the cottages, and of the house and outbuildings. I don't think the man had spent a penny on maintenance in the last few years at all. The tenant farmers are beginning to at least talk to me, now that I've had their cottages repaired in time for the worst of winter. How they survived last winter I've no idea, some of those cottages were so run down."

"I'm glad to hear that you're making progress – no-one deserves to go through winter without adequate shelter." Charlton spoke emphatically.

For both Charlton and Geoffrey, the memory of nights on cold winter ground, and peasant cottages ravaged by war, was close to the surface at that moment. Each knew, without words, what the other was thinking. After a moment's silence, Lord Geoffrey chose to turn the conversation to lighter things.

"Witherwood Chase has turned up some things rather more interesting than ugly paintings, disintegrating drapes and mouse droppings."

"Oh?" Charlton raised an eyebrow and waited for Lord Geoffrey to continue.

"Yes. Today, I decided to explore the attics – well, to start on that, at least – they are enormous, with rooms full of the discarded possessions of centuries of inhabitants. I found yet more ugly paintings – I can only assume that generations of that family had matching poor taste! But, late in the day, I found something quite wondrous." His voiced conveyed a sense of excitement that Lady Harriet had never heard in it before, and she gazed at him in some astonishment, suddenly desperate to hear more.

"There is a room up there which might best be described as a museum. A museum of perfectly cared for, neatly stored and displayed weaponry! Enough weaponry to outfit a regiment or more. I could spend weeks exploring the possibilities of what's in that room."

A boyish enthusiasm lit up Lord Geoffrey's face. Charlton smiled, caught up in the energy emanating from him.

"Well – it's yours now – you've got weeks to play with your new toys." Charlton grinned, and Lord Geoffrey laughed at his teasing.

"If only that was all I had to do! I've barely touched on the place, even though I've been digging into it for over a month now. I've made it my mission to explore every inch of it before I allow myself to indulge too much – God knows what the place has hidden in its crevices!"

As he spoke, his eyes were on Charlton's, and there was a slight emphasis on the words 'mission' and 'hidden' – an emphasis that Charlton did not miss. Unfortunately for Lord Geoffrey, Lady Harriet did not miss it either, as her adoring eyes were soaking in his every move. She found herself, when in his presence, unable to look away for too long – her eyes simply found their way back to him, as if that was the only natural place for them to rest.

She decided that there was more going on here than the apparent. And a puzzle was not something that she could leave alone. Nor was a secret. The idea of things hidden in Lord Geoffrey's house, of a potential treasure trove to be discovered, took her right back to her not-so-long-ago childhood. Before she could stop herself, words were falling from her mouth.

"Oh! I love digging through old things and finding treasures! Can I help? I am sure that Miss Carpenter would love to help too. If the house is that big and full of old things, surely more people going through them will get it done faster – and give you more time to explore those weapons." Harriet understood the value of bribery… surely he would agree to let her help, if it got him what he wanted, faster?

Lady Sylvia watched, fighting an urge to burst out laughing. The moment of what was almost terror in Lord Geoffrey's eyes did not escape her.

"Err, I... I am sure that you don't really want to get covered in dust and spider webs?" Lord Geoffrey spoke hopefully, having, for a moment, obviously forgotten that Lady Harriet was not your ordinary genteel young Lady.

Harriet laughed.

"Oh I don't mind dust and spider webs – it's no worse than I've found in the stables and the garden outbuildings, and I've been poking around in those all my life. I especially don't mind if there's something interesting to find!"

Lord Geoffrey glanced at Charlton, then at Lady Sylvia. When it was obvious that neither of them intended to rescue him, he took a deep breath, silently promising Charlton retribution for this later, and spoke.

"Well, umm..., in that case, I errr... I will be glad of your assistance, when you can spare the time. But you must be certain to bring Miss Carpenter – you must have a suitable chaperone with you, after all."

Lady Harriet tried, almost successfully, to repress her grin of triumph. Her heart beat faster at the very thought – she would get to spend whole days in his company! Surely, with such proximity, she could get him to start seeing her as a woman, not a child?

<div style="text-align:center">~~~~~</div>

Unbeknownst to Lady Harriet, at that very moment, Lord Geoffrey was most decidedly seeing her as a woman.

He had been, quite unsuccessfully, trying to avoid looking at her all evening. From the moment that he had been shown into the parlour, he had been acutely aware of her – of the sensation of her leaf green eyes following him, of the delightful shape of her beautiful body, the flushed red of her lips, the slightly dishevelled fall of her dark gold curls, that seemed never to stay quite as tidy as her maid had intended, and the subtle rich floral scent that she wore – a mixture of rose, and daphne, with perhaps a tiny touch of lemon sharpening the sweetness.

He had never met another woman who used that combination of scents – a combination that instantly took him back to the scent garden of his grandmother's house, so long ago. It made him want to simply soak it in, for it brought him a sense of peace and safety that he had not felt since his childhood years. Which felt odd to him, as, at the same time, her presence roused in him a much more carnal appreciation of everything about her. No matter how often he told himself that such an appreciation of his closest friend's sister was not a good idea, his body refused to obey his mind, and flamed into awareness the instant he found himself in the same room as the delectable Lady Harriet.

Her childlike manipulation of the conversation had charmed him, even whilst it brought him a sensation of sheer terror – for how could he possibly carry out his mission to search the house for evidence of the traitors if he was to be continuously distracted by her presence? He would have to make sure of her safety, and still somehow search, whilst concealing what he was really looking for. His head hurt at the very thought of how hard that would be.

For Lady Harriet's keen intelligence and bright curious nature would ensure that she cheerfully investigated everything…

He had been sure that Charlton would save him, but the rogue had just sat there, and let his sister gull Geoffrey into doing as she wanted. They would have words about that later!

Still, he couldn't help but be warmed by the sight of the glowing smile on her face, now that he had agreed to allow her to help. Perhaps it was worth it, to make her look that happy.

Chapter Four

The staff at Witherwood Chase has greeted the additional two footmen and the valet with suspicion, having all been working at Witherwood Chase for many years. They had their own routines, their own unstated, but agreed, divisions of authority, and had, largely, got over interpersonal politics years ago. Which wasn't to say that there were no secrets, or that they all trusted each other.

Newcomers, however, had caused them to silently close ranks and defend their territory, without any discussion required. Peterson, as one of the newcomers, was acutely aware of the wall of silence that they presented to him. Cold politeness hid secrets, but whether those secrets were a previous complicity in treason, or simply a resentment of the invasion of the place that they saw as their own, he had not yet discovered.

In time, he would do so. Baron Setford had chosen him for his skills, which included things unusual in a footman, such as weapons training, lock-picking, tracking and investigation, amongst other things.

Lord Geoffrey was a man he could respect – a man who appreciated his capabilities, and left him to get on with things. There was nothing soft or foppish about Lord Geoffrey, and his reputed skill with weapons was something any man would admire.

This evening, with Lord Geoffrey away visiting Viscount Pendholm, Peterson was using the time to apply those investigative skills of his. Most of the staff were in the servants' hall, enjoying a quiet evening. But at least two were not. After Peterson had excused himself from the gathering, supposedly to take to his bed early, he had quietly waited in a small storeroom just outside the servants' hall.

His patience was rewarded when Jobs, one of the grooms, and Ashley, one of the footmen who had long been with the house, quietly left the room. They paused a moment, not far from the storeroom door, and spoke in whispers.

"Ash, if his Lordship keeps a'diggin around like this, he's sure to be findin a door soon. Things aren't safe. Not up here. They'll have to go deep with t'others."

"Aye, but how'll we get 'em moved? Can't be a'doin it now – we don't know when His Lordship'll be back, and you'll have to be in t'stable to take his horse when he gets here."

"So I'll be in t'stable. But you go now and make sure all's still where it ought to be, and pack em up so's we can move em the next time he's away – or sooner, if'n he gets too close."

"I don't like it, but ye have the right of it, we can't do more'n that tonight."

The two moved on, from the sound of their steps in two different directions, and moments later Peterson heard the door to the back garden open as Jobs headed back to the stable. A lone set of footsteps echoed along the corridor towards the servants stairs.

Peterson eased out of the storeroom, moving along the corridor on silent feet, listening to the footfalls ahead. With great care, he followed Ashley up the servant's stairs to the floor above, and along the servants' corridor there. The corridor turned, a short distance after exiting the stairs, and Peterson paused at the corner, peeking carefully around to assess Ashley's progress. The corridor was empty. Peterson shook his head. That wasn't possible – there were no doors off this corridor for quite some distance – he couldn't have gone that far yet. Yet the corridor was empty.

Peterson eased around the corner, and walked the length of the corridor – no door, no sign of Ashley. He shook his head and took himself to his bed, mulling over what he had heard, and seen – or rather, not seen.

~~~~~

The next morning brought two visitors to Witherwood Chase. One was expected – Lady Harriet, with the long-suffering Miss Carpenter (who, unlike Lady Harriet, *did* object to dust and spider webs...) in tow, and one was unexpected, but most welcome.

Barnstable, still recovering from the shock of Lady Harriet's somewhat energetic arrival, turned in surprise at the second knock on the door.
~~~~~

Upon opening it, he discovered a sprightly gentleman of middle years, dressed in fashionable clothing better suited to a young dandy, on the doorstep. The gent stepped inside, doffed his hat, and presented his card.

Winston Featherstonehaugh Esq.

Valuer of Artworks

Bowing, he looked Barnstable in the eye and declared -

"I am here to see Lord Geoffrey Clarence. Sent, at his request, by Mr Raphael Morton. Please let his Lordship know that I have arrived."

Barnstable, rather flustered by this apparition, showed him into the visitors' parlour, and went in search of Lord Geoffrey.

Lord Geoffrey, who was just in the process of settling Lady Harriet and Miss Carpenter into the morning room, and offering her tea (whilst he worked out how on earth he was going to keep her occupied and entertained, without giving up on his own investigations completely), was as startled as Barnstable had been, when handed the gentleman's card and told of his arrival.

After the surprise wore off, however, he was rather pleased. He had written to Raphael shortly after arriving here, when he had come to the conclusion that the place was packed with horrible art, asking if he might advise on getting it valued, as a step towards disposing of it profitably. It would appear that Raphael had gone one better than simply advising, and had, before setting off on his travels, engaged a valuer on Lord Geoffrey's behalf.

How typical of Raphael! He was always generous, and often chose to simply act, rather than fuss about anything. And, perhaps, this was also a solution to occupying Lady Harriet, at least for a while, and doing so in a way where he did not have to be in her presence (and thus tortured by his awareness of her). He turned to her, smiling, and waited a moment whilst a maid delivered the tea, and left the room. Once the maid was gone, he spoke.

"Lady Harriet, might I ask you to carry out an important task for me?"

"Why of course, Lord Geoffrey – what can I do to help?"

She sounded genuinely delighted that he had a task for her, and he found himself charmed yet again by her positive, energetic nature.

"I am sure that you heard me mention, yesterday, that this house contains a vast quantity of artworks that are... not to my taste... shall we say?"

She nodded, wondering what was coming next.

"A gentleman has just arrived, whose skill is in valuing artworks. I have need of someone to go from room to room with him, and to take down notes for me on what he says about each painting, and to also make those notes very clear about the exact position of each painting, so that, later, we make no mistakes when sorting them for sale. I can provide Peterson, my footman, to be guide and escort from room to room, if you, and Miss Carpenter, will be my scribes, and capture this information for me?"

It wasn't exactly the sort of task that Harriet had hoped for, but still, it was a start. And Lady Harriet found, rather to her own surprise, that, because it was Lord Geoffrey who was asking, she was willing to take on this task, even if it sounded rather less adventurous than what she had been imagining.

"Certainly, Lord Geoffrey. I would be pleased to assist."

Had his shoulders just sagged with relief? Surely not, she pushed the thought away. That must have been her imagination at work.

"One moment."

Lord Geoffrey left the room, and went to greet Mr Featherstonehaugh. As he stepped into the room, he suddenly better understood Barnstable's reaction. The man was unusual, to say the least. Still, Raphael had recommended him. A few minutes conversation confirmed Lord Geoffrey's faith in Raphael.

However eccentric the man might appear, he seemed to know his field, providing a rapid and somewhat passionately enthusiastic assessment of the painting on the parlour wall as demonstration of his knowledge. And the number he named as a value for the painting left Lord Geoffrey a little shocked, and very pleased. If all of the paintings had similar values, he was about to be a wealthy man indeed.

After enquiring as to Mr Featherstonehaugh's arrangements, and sending a footman to pay off his driver and bring in his luggage, then to see the housekeeper about having a room prepared, he led the man into the morning room.

Upon introducing Mr Featherstonehaugh to Lady Harriet and Miss Carpenter, he was surprised to see that, within minutes, Lady Harriet had charmed Mr Featherstonehaugh, and that Mr Featherstonehaugh had charmed Miss Carpenter – which, based on his past observation of the woman, was quite an achievement! Leaving them chattering enthusiastically about the paintings on the morning room wall, he sent Peterson to fetch some pencils and suitable paper, as well as a slate to rest the paper on. Stepping back into the room he breathed a sigh of relief – perhaps his day would contain useful work after all, for the ladies appeared to be forging a firm friendship with Mr Featherstonehaugh already.

When Peterson returned, he explained the requirement, and that Peterson should, for the next few days, or until such time as the inventory was complete, place himself at Mr Featherstonehaugh and Lady Harriet's command. Given that the inventory would also need to deal with those paintings currently in the attics, which would need to be brought down for inspection, it was likely to take some considerable time.

As they set off into the house, Lord Geoffrey breathed a sigh of heartfelt relief – even though a traitorous part of him regretted letting Lady Harriet out of his sight.

<div align="center">~~~~~</div>

Lady Harriet was delighted when Lord Geoffrey actually seemed to be taking her wish to help seriously. Expecting a tedious task, and quite prepared to be a martyr to her regard for him and do it anyway, she was pleasantly surprised.

For the gentleman valuer was entertaining, passionate about his subject, and quite willing to treat a Lady's assistance with respect. He was, she suspected, the only other person that she had ever met, who was quite as… vigorous… a personality as she herself was. And, even better, Miss Carpenter appeared to actually like him! Perhaps she might not moan about the whole process after all.

Therefore, when Peterson has supplied her with pencils, paper and a slate, she was happy to leave the room and begin the apparently extensive task of cataloguing the paintings in this rather large house. Happy that is, all but a little anguished regret at not being able to stay in the same room as Lord Geoffrey, who, it seemed, had other work to do, elsewhere. She was sure that it was important. He would surely not, after all, be avoiding her company.

Chapter Five

Two sennights passed, and Christmas was upon them. It was two sennights of tedium, interspersed with moments of humour, frustration and delighted discovery. Lady Harriet, in a manner that quite astounded her family, stuck to her stated intentions, and went, accompanied by Miss Carpenter, every day, to continue the work. Such persistence, from the normally volatile Harriet, made her mother begin to think that, truly, it was possible that her *tendre* for Lord Geoffrey was more than a passing infatuation.

What astounded them all more (including Harriet herself), was that Miss Carpenter also went willingly and cheerfully, without complaint. For once she seemed to actually be happy with being dragged along by Harriet, willy-nilly. No-one mentioned either fact. But the general interest in what might be found in the rooms and attics of Witherwood Chase was high.

Lord Geoffrey was both pleased with the progress and utterly frustrated.

Pleased, because Mr Featherstonehaugh's valuation list was providing growing evidence that the dusty collection of paintings, antique furniture and tapestries in the house represented an astounding amount of wealth – even if Geoffrey only sold a small portion of them.

Frustrated, because he was still only marginally closer to fulfilling his mission for Baron Setford.

Peterson had confirmed that at least two of the staff who had come with the estate, appeared to have been party to the treasonous conspiracy, and that he suspected the house contained secret passageways or rooms. But he had been unable to find an entry, or to get enough detail of the men's involvement for Lord Geoffrey to take any action.

In addition, the daily interaction with Lady Harriet was a source of constant stress. The more he saw of her, the harder it became for Lord Geoffrey to think of her as 'Charlton's sister', and the easier it became for him to see her simply for herself – an attractive young woman, who had more determination and less fussiness about her than any other woman of his acquaintance. That she stuck at the dusty and somewhat boring work impressed him, and his respect for her grew daily. As did his attraction to her. He wanted to know more about her – how she thought, what on earth possessed her to want to do this for him, why she saw him as anything more than her brother's friend. Surely she could not still be casting him as some fairy-tale hero, based on the events of nearly a year ago?

Her scent had subtly infiltrated the house, and he was, even when in another wing of the building entirely, always aware of her.

~~~~~

They had fallen into the habit of gathering in his study each afternoon, to go over the achievements of the day – the latest finds in various rooms, as far as paintings and other items of value (for they had, some time ago, dealt with the items he had already seen, and headed into previously unexplored territory in the long unused wings of the house), the progress of repairs and renovation of many parts of the house, and the plans for the morrow.

When it was but a few days to Christmas, Mr Featherstonehaugh spoke up, after reporting his latest finds.

"Lord Geoffrey – I would like to make a pause in this work. Whilst I am keen, extremely keen, to see this through to the end – for never before have I had the privilege to assess such a remarkable collection -..." his eyes shone as he spoke, and he almost bounced on the spot, his enthusiasm still as bright as the day they had begun, "- I am also keen to return to my family for this holiday season. Now that my wife is gone, whilst they are happy in my mother's care, my children will want to see me at this time If it is agreeable to you, my Lord, I would take leave of you until just after twelfth night, then return to your most gracious hospitality to continue this work."

Whilst Lord Geoffrey felt ready to grind his teeth in frustration at the thought of another few sennights of delay to his mission, he could not, in good countenance, refuse such a request. Added to that, he, and Charlton's family, had committed to spending twelfth night at Meltonbrook Chase, where most of the other Hounds would be present.
~~~~~

He would need to devise a way to ensure that the servants suspected of being conspirators had no chance to remove anything in his absence.

"That seems, Mr Featherstonehaugh, to be an admirable plan. I must commend your good work to date, and that of Lady Harriet and Miss Carpenter in documenting your findings. I wish you the best of the season and will gladly release you to your family for now. Peterson will see to making travel arrangements for you."

He turned, unable to prevent himself, aware, as always, of Lady Harriet. She was watching him, her face a picture of conflicting emotion. Her emotions often showed on her countenance, and he was beginning to understand more of her thoughts, just from watching her face. It seemed that she felt as he did – both glad of the rest and the holiday, and reluctant to lose the excuse to spend each day, at least partly, in company with him. He most certainly felt that way with respect to her.

He had come to look forward to her arrival each day, to her bright enthusiasm lifting his spirits and to watching her sparkling green eyes light up with delight each time some new and interesting treasure was unearthed, revealed by the removal of a tattered dust sheet, or the unlocking of a previously locked chest. When she spun about exuberantly with childlike joy in the discoveries, he sometimes had to stop himself from sweeping her up and spinning with her. The impulse rather shocked him, for he had never been one for such outward show of his feelings. But stop himself he did, for he suspected that, should he take her into his arms like that, it would not stop at simply spinning about.

He was terrifyingly certain that, should he gather her to him, he would be unable to stop himself from kissing her.

At this moment, watching the flicker of sadness cross her face, followed by what seemed… could it possibly be… like longing… he wanted more than ever to kiss her. Propriety be damned. Somehow, in the last month, he had come to care for her in a new and different way. He pushed the thoughts aside and firmly repeated to himself, mentally *'Charlton's sister – not for you!'*.

Lady Harriet took a deep breath and the normal bright smile appeared on her face. She spoke politely, granting Mr Featherstonehaugh a curtsey.

"I wish you well of the season, Mr Featherstonehaugh, and your family. I will look forward to making new discoveries with you when you return."

Her words were followed by another soft voice, hesitant but clear, surprising Lady Harriet into turning slightly to look.

"As do I Mr Featherstonehaugh – this has been a most enlivening few sennights, which I have much enjoyed." Miss Carpenter actually blushed slightly as she spoke.

Lord Geoffrey and Lady Harriet shared a startled look, and both, at the identical moment, raised an eyebrow. The understanding between them was instant, and they found themselves then repressing laughter. It would seem that the usually somewhat stiff-necked Miss Carpenter had been charmed rather more than might have been expected!

Mr Featherstonehaugh swept them all a flourishing bow, thanked them for their words, and took himself off to pack.

~~~~~

As they swept up the drive of Meltonbrook Chase, Lord Geoffrey felt a little ridiculous. Here he was, arriving in his own new carriage, with a groom, two footmen and a valet. After all of those years at war, this entourage seemed excessive, yet he had no choice. He had left Walters, the other unusually skilled footman sent by Setford, at Witherwood Chase to keep an eye out for anything suspicious. With him, he had Peterson, his valet Hurst, Ashley as the second footman, and Jobs as groom and driver.

He had concluded that the simplest way to prevent his two suspect conspirators from removing evidence while he was away, was to to take them with him. They could scarcely refuse his command, but their surly expressions upon being told that they had been chosen to accompany him had seemed a good indication that Peterson's suspicions were correct.

His thoughts were brought back to the present as the house came into sight through the winter bare trees – magnificent, and imposing. And a scene of mild chaos, with multiple carriages vying for space before the doors. It would seem that everyone had arrived at once.

When he alighted from the carriage, he was swept up into exuberant greetings and laughter, leaving poor Peterson and Hurst to deal with unloading and managing the distribution of his belongings to the appropriate places, whilst he tried to keep straight all of the new faces and names through a whirlwind of introductions which only slowed down once they were all ensconced in the parlour with refreshments.
~~~~~

With a few exceptions, they were a far happier group than they had been a year ago. The year had wiped the outward traces of war from the lines of their faces, had softened the edges of their bodies a little and removed the gauntness of years of hard living, and, most importantly, had brought love and family back into their lives.

Hunter Barrington, Duke of Melton, was a transformed man – he had returned grief stricken and lost in so many ways, yet here he was with his delightful new Duchess and obviously very happy. Charlton was equally happy, and was seated beside his betrothed, Lady Odette, who, with her aunt Lady Farnsworth, had been invited to their gathering as well. Bart and Gerry were tucked away in the corner, probably talking horses – but, whilst they were the quietest in the room, and perhaps still carried the strongest after effects of the war in their minds, they too looked cheerful. Hunter's sisters, Lady Sybilla and Lady Alyse, had joined their conversation and appeared to be holding their own on the topic of horses.

The Dowager Duchess of Melton and Lady Sylvia had settled with Lady Farnsworth, and seemed deep in discussion of the plans for Charlton's wedding. The only others in the room were Lady Harriet and Miss Carpenter, Hunter's brother Charles was away, apparently dealing with estate matters elsewhere, much to his mother's displeasure.

Lady Harriet had settled on the seat of the pianoforte near the large windows to the rear of the room, her hands stroking its surface almost reverently. Miss Carpenter seemed rather lost, but, faithful shadow to Lady Harriet, she had settled on a small elegant chair off to one side, and simply watched.

It seemed wrong that Raphael was not there too. What could be so important that he would sail off and miss this gathering?

The thought was fleeting and Lord Geoffrey found himself drawn into conversation with Hunter, Charlton and their Ladies and the afternoon disappeared into the flow of discussion.

Somewhere along the way, Lord Geoffrey realised that a quiet, yet beautiful thread of melody was winding its way through the room. Not loud enough to disrupt any conversation, but soothing and relaxing in the background. He was drawn, as always to watch Lady Harriet, whose fingers on the keys were producing the marvellous sound. She seemed more still, more relaxed than he had ever seen her, and her eyes were closed – she played from memory, by feel alone, seemingly unaware of her audience, just lost in the music. He had not thought it possible for her to look more beautiful than she usually did – but like this, she was stunning.

With a start, he realised that one of the others had addressed him – had possibly spoken his name more than once.

"My apologies – I am a little... distracted."

"So I see." Hunter laughed good-naturedly and returned to the topic. "I must show you Nerissa's plans for the grounds – come spring, you won't recognise the gardens. We will have the most beautiful park of any estate in the county. But enough of us – what have you to tell us about your new estate? How goes your restoration of Witherwood Chase? I hear that it's a huge rambling place that needed quite a bit of maintenance."

"That is an accurate, if rather understated summary! It's five or six hundred years of rambling additions to the building worth of unmaintained mess."

Hunter laughed at his expression, whilst Charlton added his own commentary.

"It is, at least, an elegantly proportioned building – through all of those additions, and no matter how tangled the interior layout is, at least they managed to keep the exterior attractive!"

"True." Lord Geoffrey turned to Lady Nerissa, "I believe you would enjoy the gardens, my Lady, for the front between the wings of the house is a lovely formal pattern, and the rear, enclosed between the other wings has been a well-designed herb and scent garden. They appear to have had little good care for some years, yet retain the evidence of their design. I would be honoured should you be willing to apply your skills to helping me plan their restoration and improvement."

The young Duchess favoured him with a glowing smile which lit up her face and clapped her hands together in delight.

"Nothing would please me more, Lord Geoffrey – I will be sure to inspect them in great detail when we gather at your estate for Easter."

Conversation flowed, and Lord Geoffrey drifted from one group to another, more relaxed than he had been in months, yet always aware of the music winding through the room, his eyes drifting, again and again, back to Lady Harriet as she played.

This was something of her that he had not known, and it intrigued him that one who was normally so active and energetic could be so still and peaceful.

Eventually, dinner was announced, and Miss Carpenter stepped forward, diffidently, and gently touched Lady Harriet's shoulder, bringing her back to awareness of the room. Lady Harriet flushed, and looked rather surprised to find that so much time had passed. She stood, composed herself, and stepped forward.

Somehow, Lord Geoffrey found that he was in the perfect position to offer her his arm, and lead her in to dinner – and to discover himself seated between her, and Lady Odette. Dinner was both delightful and torture, for Lord Geoffrey was acutely aware of Lady Harriet's presence, so close beside him, her scent winding its way around him, and of the fact that he should not be reacting to her the way that he was, the way that he always did, no matter his resolve to not do so.

To add to his discomfiture, Lady Odette insisted on thanking him, yet again, for his actions in saving her life, and Charlton's, earlier in the year, even though those actions had meant the death of her father. Lady Harriet's eyes shone with that alarming hero worship again, as the story was told for those who had not been present at the time. And he had been hoping that she had stopped seeing him that way! How could he ever live up to such a perception? He was no hero, he was simply a man who did what must be done, when it was needed.

By the end of dinner, he was heartily glad to escape to the library and a glass of port with the other men.

With only Hounds present, Lord Geoffrey felt comfortable enough to discuss, a little, his mission for Setford, and his current frustrating lack of progress. They all agreed to keep an eye on the behaviour of Jobs and Ashley whilst the men were at Meltonbrook Chase. Charlton regaled them with the tale of Lady Harriet trapping Lord Geoffrey into letting her help with the exploration of Witherwood Chase, and great merriment and teasing resulted. But it was not without sympathy.

Geoffrey followed up with a description of the findings so far, including the weapons 'museum' in the attic – a find that they were all keen to see for themselves. His tales of dust sheets and mouse droppings, ugly paintings and archaic furniture were greeted with less enthusiasm, until he mentioned some of Mr Featherstonehaugh's astounding valuations of the pieces. He was slapped on the back and congratulated on his luck. In his opinion, it was only fair compensation for all his, so far fruitless, searching for hidden compartments or passages.

They settled to talking about possible places a door could be hidden, or a mechanism to unlock one, in a room or a hall. Lord Geoffrey took careful note of their ideas – anything was worth a try if it got him a step further towards finding the blasted papers for Setford.

This was the point at which, again, he missed Raphael's presence – for Raphael was the one who would have immediately 'seen' a logical plan of attack to test for, and undoubtedly find, the hidden passages. His sharp mind had always been able to lay out an approach better than any of them could.

Ah well, surely he would see Raphael at Charlton's wedding, although, God willing, by then he would have found the papers and be done with this mission.

~~~~~

Lady Harriet had excused herself from the parlour and gone in search of the necessary. That urgent business dealt with, as she returned along the hall, she heard the murmur of the men's voices through a door she was passing.

She stopped. Eavesdropping was wrong... but... she wanted to know what they spoke of... what was men's conversation about, when they were by themselves?

Feeling guilty, she applied her ear to the door. They were discussing the many ways that hidden doors and passages, rooms and compartments could be made or unlocked, in a house! What a remarkable thing to talk about. But wait... they seemed to be discussing how Lord Geoffrey could find such a thing in _his_ house! At the faint sound of a servant's footfall, imagination aflame, she stepped away from the door, and returned to the parlour.

~~~~~

Peterson, leaving Hurst to wait for Lord Geoffrey in his guest suite, went out to the stables to make sure that the carriage and horses had been suitably cared for, and to check on Ashley and Jobs.

The two had been given a small room to share in the stable block, whilst Hurst and Peterson had been given an equally tiny room in the servants' quarters of the house. With this many people, and all of their staff, in attendance, space was at a premium.

He stepped into the shadowed stables and paused. The two men were there, alone, at the far end of the row of stalls, talking quietly. Peterson froze, easing back into deeper shadow behind a rack hung with horse rugs, the scent of horses and hay rich around him, and listened. They were not speaking loudly, yet the words carried to him clearly by some trick of the building's structure.

Horses snuffled, but apart from that, there was only the men's voices to hear.

"It'll be right 'til we's back. He can't be a'searchin through the place while he's here." Ashley didn't entirely sound like he believed what he was saying.

"True, and that silly lookin' little art man's gone off home for the holiday too. So with Lord Geoffrey and Lady Harriet here we should be good."

"Still, soon's we's back, we'd better git 'em moved. 'E might find the top spot, but 'e's not like t'find the deep one."

"But Ash, what about later like. D'ye reckon any of them fancy blokes'll be ever comin' back? 'R we hidin this stuff fer nuthin?"

"Shut that thinkin Jobs! Old master paid us good to keep t'stuff safe, 'n we will. That's all there is to it."

"Right then. What'll we do if'n he gets close then? D'ye reckon as we could scare 'im off the place?"

"Not likely. 'E's a tough one – you seen 'im with them swords. Right scared me proper that. We don' wanna be buying any trouble. Just keep the stuff hid. We can worry about what to do else when we has to, 'n not afore."

At that, Jobs absently stroked the nose of the nearest horse, and the two took themselves off through the row of stalls and out the door into the grooms' quarters.

Peterson waited a few minutes, then eased out of shadow, checked on the horses, and the carriage in the next section of the building, and headed back to the house. It was good that the men had, apparently, seen Lord Geoffrey at weapons practice, and been scared by his skill. So they should be!

He was no closer to knowing what it was, exactly, that the men had hidden, but the conversation at least confirmed that it was still at Witherwood Chase, and that they wouldn't be taking it elsewhere any time soon.

They were canny, but they'd have to eventually make a mistake – one way or another, Peterson intended to find the entry to the secret passages – he was, more than ever, convinced that the papers, if that was what they were 'keeping safe' must be hidden in secret rooms or passages somewhere in the upper floors of the house. By now, there wasn't a lot of the main area of the house left unexplored, so secret places became more and more likely.

Chapter Six

With Christmas and Twelfth Night gone, Lord Geoffrey was ready to tackle the mystery of the hidden papers again. His conversations with the other Hounds had filled him with renewed determination to prod and poke at every possible piece of the walls and framing, until he found a way into the hidden passages – for he was convinced that such passages existed. What Peterson had overheard whilst they were at Meltonbrook Chase had just added to that certainty.

They were watching Ashley and Jobs closely since their return, in the hope that the two might accidentally reveal an entrance. At this instant, though, Lord Geoffrey's biggest concern was Lady Harriet. For, once the nearly complete assessment of all of the paintings and antique furniture was done, how was he to keep her occupied? If she should insist on continuing to 'help', so that she was always with him, how could he prevent her from noticing his rather eccentric looking behaviour, when he started poking and prodding at the walls of his house?

As if his thoughts of Lady Harriet had summoned her, she and Miss Carpenter arrived at that moment.

Mr Featherstonehaugh had arrived just a few hours ago, and settled in, newly enthused about his task, and keen to finish the assessment. Although, it had seemed to Lord Geoffrey, he was rather sad that it was coming to an end. He had asked, with studied casualness, if any new rooms, or storage spaces, had been discovered?

'I wish' had been Lord Geoffrey's internal thought, although he wasn't wishing for quite the same sort of new hoard of treasure that Mr Featherstonehaugh seemed to be.

Interestingly, Miss Carpenter blushed like a schoolgirl when Mr Featherstonehaugh greeted her with his customary flourishing bow and a kiss on her hand. Lady Harriet observed it with a raised eyebrow again, and said nothing.

A plan was devised, mapping out which parts of the house had yet to be checked for paintings, cleaned and set to rights, and they all set about their appointed tasks. Lord Geoffrey stood in his study, staring, unseeing, at the faded tapestry before him, as he decided where he would start.

Perhaps, given the conversations that Peterson had overheard, with mentions of down, and deep, he should work in the cellars and the servants' belowstairs rooms. It would be braving the wrath of Mrs Chester, and possibly disrupting his dinner, but it had to be done.

Days later, he was no further advanced, and had achieved little but convincing most of his staff that he was mad.

His obsessive need to have seen, touched and inspected every single corner of his home utterly puzzled them —no member of the nobility they had ever met before had given a damn about such things.

And so it went.

Mr Featherstonehaugh, with the able assistance of Lady Harriet and Miss Carpenter, and the guidance of Peterson, worked steadily through the remaining rooms, as well as the large quantity of paintings and objects which Lord Geoffrey had instructed be brought down from the attics, for their convenience.

Lord Geoffrey, with ever increasing frustration, worked steadily through the entire house, for what felt like the thousandth time, poking and prodding at walls, carvings, architraves and anything else, likely or unlikely, which might conceivably conceal a mechanism to open a hidden door or panel.

He drove the frustration from his mind by spending a few hours at the end of each day on weapons practice, trying out progressively, all of the remarkable collection of swords and other weapons that the room in the attics had provided.

Meanwhile, repairmen came and went, new items of furniture were delivered, old ones were repaired, rooms were painted, or papered with new, brighter and more appealing colours, drapes were replaced and the house was generally being brought back to the state it deserved to be maintained in.

The tenant farmer's cottages were in better condition than they had been for many years, and the farmers themselves had come from grudging politeness to cheerful respect and liking for their new Lord. Were it not for Baron Setford's mission, he could almost be happy. Almost… for a traitorous voice in his mind whispered that, without the mission, he would have no excuse to spend so much time in Lady Harriet's company.

~~~~~

A month passed, and, with only a few days' work remaining on the assessment of valuables, the neat ledgers of Mr Featherstonehaugh's findings, so ably written in Lady Harriet and Miss Carpenter's hands, showed totals so large that it made Lord Geoffrey's head spin. Gifts from Prinny might rarely come with cash attached, but this one had certainly come with more wealth included than anyone might ever have imagined.

He was now so wealthy that it might even bring him close to the wealth enjoyed by Raphael, or by Hunter, now that the mismanagement of his estates in his father's time had been corrected. It gave him great satisfaction – satisfaction that he really should not indulge in – to realise that he was now, in no way whatsoever, dependent upon his miserable brother. Alfred would be livid. He would have no leverage left, to use to try to make Lord Geoffrey behave *'as my heir should'*.

Hopefully, Raphael would be at Charlton's wedding – Geoffrey couldn't imagine him missing it, but who knew, with the sea, when ships would come in.
~~~~~

If Raphael was there, then it should be possible to get him to stay at Witherwood Chase a few days, to see the remarkable collection, and put in place a plan for its sale to the right buyers. There were, actually, a few pieces that Lord Geoffrey might keep – amongst the ugly paintings there were a small number of attractive ones – ones that Lady Harriet had expressed admiration for. Perhaps he would gift them to her.

With the wedding only a few days away, the pace of final organisation at Pendholm Hall was intense. When Charlton had decided to be married at Pendholm Hall, rather than in the crush of London as the Season began, Lord Geoffrey had been relieved.

Not only would he be able to continue his mission with less interruption, but he would not have to face the fluttering sea of hopeful young ladies seeking a wealthy war hero, who was heir to a Marquessate, to marry. Nor, whispered that part of his mind that he chose not to listen to, would Lady Harriet be surrounded by the sea of young fops who sought an heiress to marry.

The approaching wedding had, perforce, caused work to stop on the painting assessment, to a large extent. The last few rooms worth, carted down from the attics, would have to wait a week or so.

Lady Harriet and Miss Carpenter were required at the Hall to assist with the preparations, so Lord Geoffrey had asked Mr Featherstonehaugh to review his work so far and confirm his valuations as listed in the ledgers, adding some notes on which pieces he felt might sell fastest, and which pieces he believed he knew of specific potential buyers for.

With typical generosity, Lady Sylvia, upon hearing that Mr Featherstonehaugh would still be in residence, had invited him to the wedding as well.

After a hurried consultation with Peterson, Lord Geoffrey had solved the issue of how to limit the activities of their two suspect conspirators, whilst they were at the wedding, by volunteering the men to Lady Sylvia as extra help, to assist with the influx of horses, carriages and guests which would descend upon Pendholm Hall. Putting aside his annoyance with the stubbornness of his house, in not giving up its secrets, Lord Geoffrey chose, instead, to spend some time in sword work.

The weapons from the attic were fast becoming old friends, to the extent that the two swords he liked best now graced the wall of his study, in easy reach whenever he felt the need to work off his frustration.

Chapter Seven

As Lord Geoffrey dressed for the wedding, standing obediently still for Hurst to force his cravat into a complex style with military precision, he wondered what it would feel like, to want a woman so much, that you chose to marry her, and commit for life. He had seen, in both Hunter and Charlton's faces, the certainty that they had made the right choice, that happiness would be the outcome. Yet still, when he thought of the concept, what came to his mind was the image of his brother, bickering with his wife, both of them always miserable, trapped with each other forever. He shuddered.

Maybe happiness was possible – but for him? He wasn't sure. Perhaps his family was cursed. His parent's marriage had been no better than his brother's.

~~~~~

The wedding ceremony was done, and the day was drawing to a close.
~~~~~

Lady Sylvia and Lady Farnsworth had settled onto two chairs in the corner of the ballroom at Pendholm Hall, for a well-deserved rest. As they sat, watching the younger people dance, they discussed the events of the day.

The wedding had been wonderful, the celebration a success, and now Charlton and Odette were waltzing together, so obviously in love that it quite lit up the room. But wait, there, beyond them – Harriet was waltzing with Lord Geoffrey – the little minx, so she had finally persuaded him to at least look at her as a young woman. All that persistence with trudging through dusty rooms and taking notes about ugly old paintings must have achieved something for her. Lady Sylvia had to admire her daughter's sheer willpower. She was definitely beginning to think that Harriet's fascination with Lord Geoffrey had gone beyond mere infatuation, for surely, after a year, a simple infatuation would have faded.

Lady Sylvia still wasn't sure that she approved – after all, he was considerably older than Harriet, and a rather serious man – still, who knew what might come of it? He had proven himself, over this last few months, to be a man of integrity, a man who cared for his tenants, and stuck to his word. Perhaps that serious, caring nature was just what was needed as a foil to Harriet's bright volatility.

Turning further, she saw Mr Raphael Morton, the only one of the Hounds that she had not met before today. He had arrived just in time for the wedding, apparently having come almost straight from his ship, and been greeted with great joy by his fellow Hounds. She thought he looked pensive, sad, as if something troubled him, but his eyes followed Charlton and Odette wistfully. She wondered what that was about.

Lady Sylvia had liked him immediately, no matter his lack of title and the fact that he was a merchant. Any man who was a close friend of her son was welcome in her home. He was, she believed, planning to stay with Lord Geoffrey for the next few days – something to do with arranging the sale of all of those ugly paintings that Harriet had been helping to catalogue.

Her eyes found Harriet and Lord Geoffrey again, as they swirled past her on the dance floor. Harriet gazed into his eyes with that adoration which had, from the day that she had first met him, as the hero of the hour, never faded. And, most interestingly, Lord Geoffrey appeared to be gazing back into Harriet's eyes with an expression of wonder, as if he had only just discovered something new about her.

Lady Sylvia smiled to herself, well pleased with the day, all over again.

~~~~~

Lady Harriet had planned her campaign carefully. She had tracked, as subtly as she could, Lord Geoffrey's movements in the room, and made quite certain that she was close to him, when the orchestra struck up a waltz. As he looked around, apparently considering escaping the room, she had simply stepped in front of him, smiling, and waited. He had gulped, glanced around, and apparently, having now known her for some time, concluded that she had, yet again, trapped him neatly. He had offered her his hand, raised an enquiring eyebrow, and, at her nod of acceptance, swept her on to the floor.
~~~~~

She looked stunning. Her gown of a vibrant rich green (a colour officially unsuited to so young a woman, according to the disapproving old biddies of the *ton*) made her eyes shine, and made their green even brighter. Her rich dark gold hair was swept up into a pile of artful curls, which tumbled to the side, drawing the eye to her shoulders and the creamy expanse of her décolletage. His eyes were most happy to be led there.

As he took her into his arms, her unique scent surrounded him, a scent which he found arousing, yet the scent of safety, of home, of childhood delight. After the long day, and a glass or two of celebratory wine, she was intoxicating to his tired senses. He wanted to kiss her. He had known, for so long now, that should he take her into his arms, he would want to do just that. He forced himself to remain a gentleman, guiding her through the flow of dancers, letting the swirling steps of the waltz carry them smoothly around the room. She was light on her feet and sure, seeming made to fit against him, somehow perfectly matched, even though he was large and tall, and she was quite petite of height, and slim.

She was gazing into his eyes, her face full of that adoration that he found so alarming, however flattering it might be to be regarded as a hero. He found himself gazing back, and the room faded away around them, until it seemed it was only them, and the music. Her eyes, seen close up like this, were a mixture of shades of green, like sunlight through leaves in spring, and they shone with her pleasure in the moment. He was lost in their depths. How had he ever thought her a child? Once, that might have been the case, but no more. The woman he held in his arms was well shaped and grown, and well aware of her own desires.

In that moment, even the fact that what she desired was him, suddenly seemed less frightening. But, cold reason insinuated itself into the moment, she was still Charlton's little sister! He should not be looking at her like this, with eyes that heated with desire, that traced her delectable lips and wished to kiss them. He needed to escape, or he would, of a certainty, do something he would forever regret. As soon as the waltz ended he would deliver her back to that companion of hers, and find Raphael.

As if the thought had magically caused her to appear, he saw Miss Carpenter. But she wasn't standing patiently on the sidelines, as was usually expected of a companion and chaperone. She was swirling past them on the floor, in the arms of none other than Mr Featherstonehaugh. Well, if that was the lay of the land, things might soon be most interesting!

$$\sim\sim\sim\sim\sim$$

Harriet had lost all sense of time and place. The feeling of being in Lord Geoffrey's arms was better, oh so much better, than anything she had imagined. She gazed into his dark storm grey eyes and simply soaked up the moment. She knew well that her heart was quite likely on her face, her feelings spelled out for anyone to see, and she didn't care one whit. So long as he saw and did not instantly abandon her, she could cope.

His eyes connected with hers, and the warmth, and... was that desire?... that she saw in them made her heart race and her breathing come short. She had no idea how long the music played, only a wish for it to never end.

But, of course, it did.

He had appeared as caught up in the moment as she, but as the music stopped, he swirled her to the side, and quickly delivered her to Miss Carpenter's company, before bowing elegantly.

"Thank you, Lady Harriet. If you will excuse me, I must have a word with Mr Morton."

He turned, leaving her feeling somewhat lost and bereft, and walked away from her rapidly, as if escaping some terrible fate. Her mouth fell open in shock a moment, before she forced her best bright smile back onto her face. How could he? How mortifying! She had thought, for a little there that he... but no, obviously not.

She was still determined. There was hope. She would not give up. There was no-one else for her. She would convince him yet.

Chapter Eight

Three months! He had been searching through the entirety of the damn house for three whole months now! It had delivered him enormous riches in artworks, antique furniture, tapestries and trinkets. It had provided a magnificent collection of weapons. It had delivered him a new perspective on the world, and a new sense of self-worth, as he restored farmers' lives, as well as their cottages. It had delivered him the delicious torture of seeing Lady Harriet nearly every day. But the one thing it had not delivered him was the papers that Baron Setford required him to find.

And now he was at wits end. He could not imagine where else to look, yet he had not found the secret passageways or any other hidden spaces. And today, Mr Featherstonehaugh had finished the last of his assessment. In a few scant minutes, he, Peterson and the Ladies would appear in this very room to report the final discoveries.

What was he to do once that was done?

Raphael had been amazed at the paintings and other objects, and had readily agreed to arrange sale of the items. The first shipment was packed, and would be collected tomorrow, or the following day, by a specialist carrier that Raphael had engaged to transport it to his London warehouse.

Raphael had raised an eyebrow at Lady Harriet's involvement in the search and assessment of the contents of the house, but Lord Geoffrey had studiously ignored the implied question. Raphael let him be, but went away looking very thoughtful. So everything was in order. Everything except the reason that he was here in the first place, the reason that he had been given the place. The place that he had now made his home. What was he to do?

Barnstable chose that moment to knock, and ushered Mr Featherstonehaugh and the Ladies into the room, closely followed by a maid with the tea tray. Barnstable was becoming remarkably attuned to his habits, and he nodded his gratitude to the man as he quietly left the room.

"Lord Geoffrey. Today has been a quite marvellous conclusion to this work." The man's voice vibrated with excitement, despite his surprisingly bedraggled appearance. Obviously, he had managed to discover one of the last remaining caches of dust and mouse droppings in the house!

"We discovered another twenty paintings, in a tiny store room near the entry to the servant's stairs, just down the hallway here. And they are magnificent. I believe at least two to be by renowned masters, pieces thought lost to the world, now recovered! They alone may be worth nearly as much as all of the others together."

If Lord Geoffrey had been stunned by the wealth found so far, this statement tipped him into a state of total incomprehension of the numbers involved.

Then, quite spoiling the effect of his pronouncement, Mr Featherstonehaugh sneezed – violently and repeatedly. Miss Carpenter rushed to his side, concern writ large on her face. She proffered a dainty handkerchief, which he gratefully took.

"I must apologize – the dust you see – in my excitement I managed to pull the entire dust sheet down on me, from the largest canvas. I fear my attire is not at its best, nor are my nasal passages. If you will excuse me, I will go and change." He took himself from the room, Miss Carpenter fussing at his side.

Lord Geoffrey found himself alone with Lady Harriet, and a short but difficult silence ensued. Dragging her eyes from his, she spun away, looking for whatever distraction was available. There, right in front of her, across the room, was a large faded tapestry.

Why had she never noticed it before? They had certainly not yet listed it on their inventory. Stepping forward, she examined it closely. It was certainly old, but appeared to be of exquisite workmanship. The threads were unfrayed, the edges mostly firm.

It seemed, to her untrained eye, to be simply in need of a careful cleaning. There was so much dirt on it that, in parts, the picture was hard to make out. Stepping forward again she lifted one side of it, studying the only spot that she could see where the edge did seem a little frayed – as if that spot had been touched more than any other part of it.

As she stepped, her foot caught on the edge of the rug, and she stumbled against the wall, one hand tugging on the tapestry, and the other slamming into the whorl of carving on the top of the wainscoting beside it.

Except that the wall seemed to have suddenly become insubstantial, for she kept tumbling forward. Lady Harriet gasped and righted herself, just as Lord Geoffrey reached her and took firm grip on her shoulders to stop her fall.

Even in her moment of shock, she felt the warmth of his touch and a little burst of joy ran through her. He cared enough to catch her!

At the same second, they both realised what had happened, what they saw before them. For the wall had opened. The tug on the tapestry had caused it to slide to one side, and the hit on the whorl of carving had somehow opened a door – a door which swung inwards to a narrow passage. Their eyes met, and his lit with such joy that she knew there was something important about the opening wall, some secret.

But, when he whooped, and swept her into his arms to spin her around in an exuberant display of delight, she quite forgot about anything else but his touch, at least until he put her down again.

"Uhh, I apologize, that was uncalled for, but… I have been looking for something like this – I was so sure that the house had secrets yet to show us, and I was right! And you, most cleverly, have found it!"

He pulled her to him again for a moment, and kissed her full on the lips. She melted against him, heat flooding through her body.

If this was how he reacted to secret doorways, she would endeavour to discover one every day! Then he released her and stepped back, seeming suddenly embarrassed by his actions.

Lord Geoffrey looked into her flushed face, and wanted to kiss her again. He did not – what he had already done was unforgiveable, no matter how much he wanted to repeat it. She was not for him. Quickly, he turned to the matter in hand – the door in the wall. Grabbing a small decorative stone urn off a side table, he used it to ensure that the hidden door could not close, before stepping inside the space.

"Perhaps a lantern… or at least a candle… would be useful? Lady Harriet's voice penetrated his excited contemplation of what he saw. She was correct. He turned, to find her already offering him a lit taper. Resourceful as always.

The light showed that the space within the walls was not large. It appeared to be a small room, not a passage at all. He felt a moment of crushing disappointment – he had been sure it would be more than this! Perhaps it was. He set to examining it minutely. One end of the space appeared to be a cabinet built into the wall – that was the side towards the windowed wall – which made sense, for there was nowhere in that direction for a passage to fit.

The cabinet door was, as could be expected, locked. He huffed his disappointment again, turning to examine the rest of the small space. Nothing of significance that he could see. Lady Harriet peered in through the door.

"Oh, a cabinet. Is it locked?"

"Yes, unfortunately, it appears to be quite solidly locked – and no sign of a key."

She nodded, and squeezed in beside him. His body tightened at the press of hers against him and he gasped. She crouched, putting her face at a level with the lock (and also, alarmingly for his peace of mind, at a level with certain parts of his anatomy, which were very aware of her presence). She pulled a hairpin from her tangled locks as she did so.

"Hold the light down here please."

Shocked, he did as requested, and watched in open admiration as she swiftly picked the lock.

"How… Where… did you learn to do that?"

She looked back at him, flushing, perhaps embarrassed?

"I… when I was a child, Michael – my horrible, now deceased elder brother, you remember? Michael used to lock away anything I treasured, just to be mean – he was like that. So I learned to pick locks to get my things back. Jimmy taught me. He was our stable boy in London. I think he'd been a thief before we took him on. But he never stole from us."

"Lady Harriet, I am doubly indebted to you. And impressed by your resourcefulness."

She flushed again, definitely embarrassed this time, at receiving praise from him, and squeezed her way back out of the space to allow him to investigate the contents of the cabinet.

The brush of her body against him brought a new rush of desire, but he pushed it aside. Right now, the contents of that cabinet were his first priority.

She took the candle from his fingers, and held it for him, so that his hands were free to pull forth the roll of pages within. Shaking, he unrolled it. And, for a few moments, was hit hard by disappointment again. Not a set of incriminating letters or lists. Just a collection of maps or diagrams.

And then his brain caught up with what he was seeing. In his hands was a full set of maps of his house – every floor, of every wing, and the attics, and the cellars. Neatly drawn, well noted with names of rooms, and with some odd symbols in various places. Most importantly, these maps showed a large number of passages and rooms that were not part of the normally accessible parts of the house. It appeared that he held a full set of maps showing the hidden passages and rooms in the house, and under it.

This was a prize indeed. He stepped back out into the study, and allowed the hidden door to close, after carefully studying the mechanism. Then he opened it again, to be sure that he could, closed it, and took the maps to his desk.

Lady Harriet followed, her face alight with curiosity.

In that instant he realised – there was no going back now, no keeping her out of it – she had found the secret, opened the door, unlocked the cabinet – she knew that the maps existed. After all that, she had a right to see them. But what could he tell her, without revealing the detail of his mission?

Thinking carefully about that very pertinent question, he spread the maps out on the desk. They were old, and appeared to have been added to and annotated at various times over many years. He wondered who had first drawn them. Whoever they were, he owed them a debt of gratitude.

Lady Harriet stood close and peered over his shoulder to better see the detail. The brush of her body against him, the touch of a tendril of hair against his cheek, made him nearly groan aloud. He forced his mind back to the drawings in front of him. The longer he looked, the more excited he became.

There were, it seemed, secret passages and rooms on every floor except the ground floor. After some thought he concluded that one of the symbols used indicated the locations of doors into the passages. He was not entirely sure about some of the other symbols, but perhaps they might indicate the locations of peepholes, which would permit a person lurking in the walls to spy on the occupants of the normal rooms? It was a likely possibility.

By far the most fascinating thing was the drawing of the cellars. For, not only was there a sheet for the level of the cellars he knew of, where root vegetables and wines and other comestibles were stored, but there was another sheet, which appeared to show not just one, but two further levels of cellars below that. At this rate, he would be spending the next few weeks exploring secret rooms and passages, and still be lucky to get through all of them!

And... if the conspirators knew of these, if, as Peterson had surmised, they had hidden the treasonously incriminating papers somewhere in this warren of hidden passages, what action might they feel forced to take, once they realised that he was exploring them??

Chapter Nine

With a start, Lady Harriet pulled back, removing the contact between her, and Lord Geoffrey. She could still feel the heat of him, as if they yet touched. What she truly wished was to throw herself into his arms, to regain that moment when he had kissed her. Instead, she stepped back, considering the maps of the house, and what they had just revealed. She wondered how the mechanisms for the other doors worked.

The thought of exploring the passages was beyond exciting – who knew what they might find within, given what had been there to find in the open parts of the house!

"When will we…"

"No-one must know of…"

They both spoke at the same instant, and stopped at the same instant, startled. He was the first to recover his composure.

"No-one must know of this. It must be kept between us for now."

"Why?"

And here was the moment. The moment that he was still not truly prepared for. What could he say? Could he trust her with the truth? Or would that simply endanger her more than this knowledge already did? Her bright green eyes watched him, waiting.

He gulped for air, his throat suddenly tight, and made an impetuous decision, perhaps an unwise one, yet it seemed, in the moment, the only decision to make.

"Because, my dear Lady Harriet, these hidden rooms and passages may, nay, almost certainly do, contain evidence of treason against the crown, perpetrated by the previous owner of this house, and an unknown number of other conspirators. Some of whom are, I believe, still here in the house, in my employ. If they were to realise that we have discovered this, they might choose to act precipitously. Speaking of this would be to endanger your life."

Her face had paled as he spoke, and she stared at him in some shock. But her eyes shone with intelligence, and it seemed that she was thinking, rather than about to faint away in a ladylike swoon. Minutes passed, while she absently twirled a tendril of hair around her finger, and thought, then she spoke.

"I see. If that is the case, then we will simply have to take the utmost care as we explore them. For surely, whatever is hidden there is what you have been seeking this last three months. This information makes sense of your insistence on seeing every crevice of the house – am I correct in my deduction?"

She showed no sign of fear, and her usual enthusiasm for life was undimmed – before him, what he saw was excitement.

She was quite a remarkable woman.

In that instant, he realised that she had just, neatly, trapped him again – for he had no choice but to allow her assistance, if he wished to ever complete his mission. She would get what she wanted, in this, at least.

"Yes, you are correct. That is what I have searched for, and yes, I must reluctantly allow you to assist me in searching these hidden passages. I have already stepped beyond the bounds of what I should reveal to you, and, if Charlton knew of this, he would never forgive me for involving you, but I see that I have little choice. For now, I must lock these away in my own safe, before anyone sees them. Miss Carpenter is sure to soon realise that she has left you scandalously unchaperoned, and return in a fluster!"

He stood, and went to a small cabinet near the desk, opening compartments and locks to secure the plans. Lady Harriet had, until then, quite completely forgotten about Miss Carpenter, and prayed that her *tendre* for Mr Featherstonehaugh would keep her distracted a little longer.

"Then how will you explain to me what we must do? How will we plan, if we are never to be alone?"

It was an excellent question, to which Lord Geoffrey was sadly lacking an answer. All manner of thoughts flooded his mind, in the context of being alone with Lady Harriet.

None of them had the least to do with his mission.

He forced the inappropriate thoughts aside and considered.

"Perhaps, tomorrow, you should ride here, rather than take the carriage. I could then take a little time out from ugly paintings and dust to show you around the property – I believe that you have yet to see the extent of the grounds in the direction away from Pendholm Hall?"

She nodded, waiting for him to continue.

"Of course, Miss Carpenter would accompany us, for reasons of propriety. It would, I am sure, not prevent her chaperonage from being effective, even if her lamentable riding abilities meant that we were well ahead of her most of the time – not out of sight, but certainly out of earshot."

Lady Harriet's face lit with delight and amusement. So, he had noticed her rather naughty tendency to make poor Miss Carpenter struggle to keep up with her when riding! It was a very clever solution, especially as she loved to ride, and, now that the weather was warming, she would enjoy a chance to see the grounds. It would be the perfect way to talk privately. And Moonbeam needed the exercise after the last few months when Harriet had sadly neglected her to spend her time at Witherwood Chase.

"What a brilliant idea!" She clapped her hands together, and spun across the room, all energy and impatience for the morrow. At that precise instant, Miss Carpenter, looking flushed, embarrassed and guilty, all at once, entered the room. Finding Lord Geoffrey and Lady Harriet on opposite sides of the room, and most obviously not engaged in anything scandalous, she breathed a sigh of relief, and chose to say nothing. Lady Harriet smiled, and her eyes lit with devilment.

"Miss Carpenter! We are to have a treat tomorrow. Lord Geoffrey has most kindly invited us to ride over, and he will ride with us to show us the farthest reaches of the Witherwood Chase grounds. Is that not most delightful, after all of these days amongst dusty paintings?"

Miss Carpenter paled, then squared her shoulders with a long-suffering sigh.

"Delightful indeed, Lady Harriet." Her tone was dry, and Lord Geoffrey looked at her in surprise. Perhaps the companion was not so mousy as he had supposed.

~~~~~

All around, the ride was a great success. Miss Carpenter, whilst not exactly happy about it, managed to cope quite well, and was just slow and sedate enough to allow them the perfect opportunity to talk. Lord Geoffrey discovered himself having fun, even whilst discussing a topic of such a serious nature.

Lady Harriet rode extraordinarily well, and Lord Geoffrey thrilled to the chance to ride with a woman who could not only keep up with him, but potentially even outride him. He explained, in as minimalist a way as possible, that he was working secretly for a representative of the crown, to find and neutralise the last of the treasonous conspirators. That he was searching for a cache of incriminating papers, and possibly other items, and that Ashley and Jobs seemed the only possible guilty parties amongst the staff that had come with the house.
~~~~~

He also explained that Peterson, Walters and Hurst were to be trusted absolutely, but that everyone else was not. The difficulty was going to be finding a way that Lady Harriet might assist in the search, whilst staying within the bounds of propriety. The only possible option seemed to be taking Miss Carpenter into their confidence. A step that Lord Geoffrey was loath to take, for every extra person who knew was another person at risk.

In the end, they agreed to think on that for a few days, whilst Lord Geoffrey studied the maps, and began to identify the places in the rooms and corridors, which corresponded to the points on the map marked with the symbol which they believed to represent doors. For they had to find those locations, before they could work out how to open the doors.

Lady Harriet prayed that all of the doors would have similar mechanisms, for if they did not, the search would be slow and difficult.

Chapter Ten

Three days later, Lord Geoffrey was ready to start opening doors – if he could work out how. He was fairly certain that he had discovered the doors, less certain of the mechanisms controlling them. Lady Harriet, unable to bear the thought of missing out on exploring, approached Miss Carpenter carefully.

Fifteen minutes later, a combination of appealing to Miss Carpenter's patriotic nature (which was not difficult, as her father and brother had both perished as soldiers in the war) and threatening to tell Lady Sylvia of her *tendre* for Mr Featherstonehaugh, and the hour that she had spent in his company, leaving Lady Harriet unchaperoned, had persuaded Miss Carpenter to co-operate.

Once convinced, Miss Carpenter was surprisingly enthusiastic about the project, for which Lady Harriet was immensely grateful. The plan was simple, and still rather risky, but it was the best they could do. Miss Carpenter would continue to work with Mr Featherstonehaugh, sequestered in the library, working through his final notes.

They would all pretend that Lady Harriet was also working with them, and, if asked by a servant, or anyone else, Miss Carpenter would report that Lady Harriet had simply left the room to use the necessary. Miss Carpenter was quite confident that Mr Featherstonehaugh would, because she asked it of him, also ask no awkward questions.

Meanwhile, Lady Harriet and Lord Geoffrey would be exploring the passages. The doors, between the map allowing them to be found, and the fact that the mechanisms were all very similar – in each case there was a whorl of carving of some sort to push, and a drape, tapestry or painting to pull on, at the same time – proved remarkably easy to open. Lord Geoffrey felt rather foolish that he and Peterson had not found even one of them in those three long months of searching – they seemed so obvious now that he knew what to look for!

~~~~~

Over the next two sennights, Lord Geoffrey and Lady Harriet discovered two things – that lurking in corridors and poking at walls, then disappearing through them, was remarkably difficult to do without drawing the notice of servants, and that hidden passages contained even greater amounts of dust and mouse droppings than long unused rooms. What they did not discover, was the cache of incriminating treasonous documents which they sought.

It also became, as they worked at checking the passages and tiny hidden rooms, at first together, and then separately, obvious that there were more passages than those shown on the maps - which depressing fact just made the work harder.
~~~~~

There were moments of amusement, and moments of great surprise, as they discovered yet more paintings and other minor valuables, long forgotten in recesses in the hidden rooms and passages, or looked through peepholes to discover which rooms they allowed one to spy on.

Lady Harriet took especial delight in discovering a peephole which let her spy on Miss Carpenter and Mr Featherstonehaugh. They were studiously working away, whilst each casting surreptitious longing glances at the other, when they though the other wasn't looking. It took enormous effort for Lady Harriet not to burst into a fit of the giggles watching them. More seriously, she took note of all of the rooms for which she found peepholes, and they compared them to the symbols on the maps. It seemed that they had guessed the symbol correctly.

Each day provided another chance for Lady Harriet to be as close to Lord Geoffrey as she could manage, without actually throwing herself at him. Which was what, if she was honest, she truly wished to do. Now, more than ever, he took her breath away. Not only was he heroic by his actions, but also by his nature. His steadfast refusal to take advantage of their scandalous proximity, even whilst his storm grey eyes followed her and, in unguarded moments, revealed what she dared to hope was desire for her, was demonstration of his honourable character.

She found his dedication to his mission, and his willingness to suffer months of dirt, dust and tedium impressive, and worthy of respect. Especially when compared to the town fops who had clung to her side this Season past.

Still, for both of them, the lack of result for their efforts was wearing, as was the continual subterfuge required to keep their actions secret. By the end of the second sennight, the novelty of peepholes and hidden passages had quite worn off, and frustration had set in.

~~~~~

As it happened, their explorations had not gone entirely unnoticed. Late one evening, after Lady Harriet and Miss Carpenter had returned to Pendholm Hall, and Lord Geoffrey had locked himself away in his study, with the maps, and a glass of good brandy, two figures slid quietly through the shadows at the back of the house. They made no sound until they reached the run down shepherd's cottage at the edge of the boundary woods.

Once inside, by the light of an only partially unshuttered lantern, Ashley and Jobs looked at each other with fear on their faces.

"What'll we do Ash? He's found the passages – least some of 'em anyway. The dust's all disturbed and some of them old pictures in there's been moved." Jobs' voice quavered as he spoke.

"We'll move them things from up top down with the rest tomorrow – one way or t'other - we can't wait any longer. I don't think he's found the hidden door down the bottom – even if'n he has, he won't find the second one." Ashley put as much confidence as he could into the statement, but, in truth, he wasn't sure it was true.
~~~~~

"What if he does? What if'n we runs inta him in the passages?"

"Then we'll deal with it. Whatever it takes. If he catches us, we're dead – we'll hang or worse for those papers. If'n he finds us, he'll have an 'accident' – I'll make sure of it."

"I dunno about that. I nivver signed up fer no killin. But... if'n it's his neck or mine..."

"Exactly Jobs, exactly. I'll send a message ter Nobby first thing. Have him ready to cart off whatever might need to be... removed, if'n ye take me meaning."

"Aye, that be best then. Nobby won't be askin' any questions, 'n if'n he's not needed, no-one'll know."

They talked for a while longer, about the best way to get from the top passages to the very bottom, without being seen, or making any noises in the wrong places.

Finally, satisfied that they'd done all they could to prepare, they disappeared back into the night.

~~~~~

Lord Geoffrey locked the maps away again, satisfied with the day's work. There were only two areas of the upper floors hidden passages left to search – even allowing for possible extra bits that weren't marked on the maps. Tomorrow Lady Harriet would take the top floor, just below the attics, and he would take the one below. Surely they would find the papers in one of those two places.
~~~~~

If not, they would move on to the cellars. Which would be more difficult, for access to those meant moving into the servant's' domain, and staying unnoticed would be nigh on impossible. He prayed that would not be necessary. Every day of this work was more fraught with the risk of discovery.

His admiration for Lady Harriet's resourcefulness, determination and persistence had grown with every day of the search. Had she truly been still the tantrum prone child that Charlton had described to him so often, she would have long ago lost patience with the whole thing. But she had not. She had stayed true to her commitment to helping him, and applied her keen intelligence to searching, and to their efforts to update the maps as they did so.

And every day he spent in her company, especially when they had searched together in the tight confines of the passageways, it became harder and harder to convince himself that he should not be attracted to her.

She was like no other woman he had ever met. When she gathered up Miss Carpenter and went home at the end of each day, he found himself oddly bereft. The house felt infinitely emptier without her bright presence. He pushed those thoughts away, for the thousandth time, and went back to considering what he would do when they did, finally, find the damn papers.

It startled him to realise that he had no idea exactly what those papers would contain. No doubt Setford had a very clear idea. Which was all that mattered. Lord Geoffrey couldn't wait to find the things, pass them to Setford, along with his traitorous employees, and be done with the mission.

He had come to like Witherwood Chase, to feel at home there, in a way that he had not felt at home anywhere since he was a boy of eight or ten, and his parents and grandmother had still been alive.

He wanted the dark stain of treason gone from the place, to make it completely his.

He wanted that done before the rest of the Hounds, and their families, came to stay at Eastertide, so that it might be a time of joyous celebration of the bonds they shared, with no shadow hanging over it.

Chapter Eleven

Lady Harriet was determined. This was the day when she would find what they sought, and bring this tedious process to an end. *'But'*, whispered the stubborn small voice in her mind *'how will you then find cause to see Lord Geoffrey?'* She ignored it. That was a problem for another day. For now, Lord Geoffrey desired to find those papers, so searching for them was her first priority.

She stood in a small parlour on the upper floor, with windows which overlooked the herb and scent garden in the rear courtyard area of the house. This wing was one of the oldest parts of the house, and, along this side of the floor, the rooms all opened into each other, in the manner of centuries past, with the doors close to the windows in each case. The centre of the floor contained servants' corridors, but also secret passages, accessed through the apparently blank walls which faced the windows in each room. At the far end of the floor, there was an area which was not clearly explained by the maps.

Lady Harriet held high hopes for what that area might contain. Once certain that no-one was near, she stepped to the rear of the room and, with careful coordination, shoved hard on a carved leaf at the edge of the mantle above the fireplace, whilst also pulling on a shelf of the adjoining bookcase. The shelves pivoted out to her pull, and she stepped into the dark passageway revealed, partially unshuttered her small lantern, and pulled the door closed behind her, taking careful note of the placement of the lever which would allow her to open it later.

She worked her way down the passage, looking through peepholes, poking into crevices, seeking any evidence of other doors, of cabinets skilfully laid into the walls, or of any other possible hiding places. For a long distance, there was nothing of interest beyond the peepholes. Eventually, she reached what appeared to be an end to the passage. Frowning, she retraced her steps to the last peephole. Looking through it confirmed her suspicions – the passage should continue, for the room she saw was the second to last room on the floor, not the last.

Returning to the blank wall, she ran her fingers over its surface, and traced its edges, as well as the walls to either side. Finally, when she was beginning to think that she might be wrong, that the passage might simply end, her gloved fingers caught on an uneven area of the side wall. A few moments poking and pushing at it experimentally, and the blank end of the passage shifted slightly, with a soft click. She pulled it open and slipped through, impatiently pulling at an errant tendril of hair as it caught on the door frame.

~~~~~

Jobs had come into the kitchen for a quick bite of food, taking advantage of the left-overs from the nobility's luncheon. He turned away, as if about to return to the stables, catching Ashley's eye as he did so. At Ashley's quick nod, Jobs stepped out of the kitchen, but, when sure that there were no eyes upon him, went quickly up the servants' stairs, rather than out the side door to the stables. Not long after, Ashley also quit the kitchens and casually took the same path.

One floor up, they took separate ways, Jobs slipping into the walls as soon as possible, but Ashley continuing in the servants' corridors, looking for all the world just like any footman might, going about his appointed business. Closer to the end of the old wing, he also slipped into the walls, finding Jobs waiting. In careful silence, they climbed up another two floors of narrow hidden stairs.

They emerged into a dusty room, tucked right at the end of the wing, close below the attics. Unlike most of the hidden spaces, this had a tiny amount of natural light from a narrow strip of dusty window.

From outside the house, it seemed just another window in the row along that floor, a bit smaller for being right at the end, but nothing unusual. From the inside, it let in just enough light, past the aged velvet drape that hung over it, to show a tiny table, a single chair, a rough pallet on the floor and a small crate in one corner. On the crate stood a pitcher of water, and some battered cups, just below an odd looking tap on the wall.
~~~~~

The room was just below the rainwater cistern – as a bolt hole, it had the superior advantage of a water supply. Incongruously, beside the crate stood a largish basket full of dirty looking dust sheets, topped by a tangle of old ropes or curtain pulls.

"Right then, let's be about it." Ashley strode across the room and lifted the rough timber tray with the pitcher and cups. Setting it on the small table, he turned back to the crate. A few minutes work, and the apparently nailed together crate was in two pieces, revealing a smallish strongbox nestled at its core. The box was old, of ebony or some similar wood, banded in iron. It was locked, and heavy.

Jobs had pulled half the dust sheets from the basket, and Ashley carefully settled the box in amongst the remaining ones, and set to reassembling the crate, whilst Jobs reached for the dust sheets to cover the box. A sound shocked them to stillness. Their eyes met, with fear their uppermost emotion.

The other entry to the room – a secret door, behind a secret door, at the far end of a hidden passage, a door that no-one else should be able to find, opened, and Lady Harriet stepped through. The dim light from the window was enough to momentarily blind her after the deep darkness of the passageway, and she stood, blinking in confusion at the sight of the two men before her.

Ashley recovered from his shock first, and, just as Lady Harriet's eyes fell upon the box, and lit with startled comprehension of its importance, Ashley grabbed her, clamping one hand across her mouth, and the other around her body, trapping her arms against her sides. He hauled her back against him.

"Jobs!" Ashley's voice broke Jobs from his shock, and he leapt forward to grab Lady Harriet's legs before she could try to get away. Five minutes later, Ashley and Jobs bore bruises and scratches from Lady Harriet's failed attempts to escape.

They stood back, breathing hard from the effort, whilst Lady Harriet lay on the pallet, bound and gagged, her dress a little torn, and her eyes blazing her anger at them as clearly as if she could speak. If looks were daggers, they would both have been dead.

"Guess we'll be needin' Nobby then." Ashley's voice was flat, but not displeased. Rather be found by this little piece than by his Lordship with his bloody swords or a pistol. This way, they'd turn a nice profit too. Nobby had contacts. There'd be a few competing to buy something this pretty, if he wasn't mistaken. The high class houses of pleasure had a taste for quality fresh goods like her. They'd just have to be sure they got her out and gone tonight, and kept it so no-one suspected them.

But who would? She must have found the entry to this room by blind luck — and if she was alone, that meant no-one else knew where she was. For now, she could stay right there on the pallet, while they got the other valuables stowed away in the deep.

"Let's be getting this down t' the deep then. Once tis stored away with t'other, we c'n worrit about mileddy here."

Jobs piled the scattered dust sheets over the box, throwing aside the few pieces of old rope which had not been used in binding Lady Harriet, and Ashley lifted the basket. He looked at Lady Harriet, a touch regretfully.

"We'll be a seein' you later mileddy. Tis a pity we'll get a better price for ye untouched, or I'd be a tastin' the wares before we ship em, if'n ye understands me."

~~~~~

Lady Harriet watched as they exited the room, through a tiny door near the window. She'd think about the meaning of those words later. For now, once she was sure that they were gone, she would concentrate on trying to escape.

Lying still, she listened carefully. Their steps receded – it sounded as if there were stairs beyond that door. And then there was silence. Drifts of disturbed dust floated in the air, turned to sparkling gold by the faint rays of afternoon sun coming through the tiny window. She would have thought it pretty, were her situation not so dire.

Once their footsteps faded into the silence, she let herself move. She pulled and twisted her hands and feet, but only succeeded in abrading her wrists and ankles on the rough bits of rope that they had bound her with. She panted for breath, revolted by the taste of the dusty cloth that filled her mouth. She refused to think about what that taste might be caused by. She would especially not contemplate any thought whatsoever of mouse droppings. Definitely not.

Shouting was impossible, and anyway, it was extremely unlikely that anyone would be near enough to hear – for this was the furthest end of the least used wing of the house, and behind three layers of secret doors as well.
~~~~~

She could but hope that Lord Geoffrey would become alarmed when she did not return for their late afternoon discussion of the day's achievements, and would come seeking her. The hours between now and then loomed ahead of her, an interminable opportunity for despair.

Resting before another attempt at loosening the ropes, she finally allowed herself to consider the import of the footman's parting words. Try as she might to discover another, she could only find one possible meaning in what he'd said.

She might be physically an innocent, but she was certainly not ignorant about what men did with women, or of the existence of places expressly for allowing men to satisfy those needs. Her deceased elder brother, terrible man that he had been, had made quite certain of that by his actions. When her mother had, after his death, rescued the girls that he had abused and left with child, Lady Harriet had discovered many things that she might have wished not to know.

She loved Mary, Polly and Sally, and their children, just as much as she would have had they been legitimate, and so did her mother, for her brother's behaviour had certainly not been the fault of the girls. But, being of curious mind, she had asked them, once they trusted her, about their experiences. Their answers had been quite an education.

And, applying the understanding gained from those conversations to the footman's words, she was left with a single stark conclusion. Those men were going to take her somewhere, and sell her to a house of pleasure, to be used by men, against her will. The thought terrified her.

She well knew that, if there was love, or even respect, between a man and woman, as was the case with Charlton and Odette, and had been the case with her mother and father, when he still lived, then the physical activities carried out between men and women could be acceptable, or even pleasant.

But she also knew, from what her terrible brother had done to the girls, that it could be very unpleasant indeed.

She lay there shaking, exhausted by her struggles and close to tears. But she refused to give up hope. After all, this room was at the top of the house. They still had to get her out unseen – which would mean late at night.

So, there was time. Time for her to think, time for her to keep working at the ropes, and, she fervently prayed, time for Lord Geoffrey to find her. He was a hero. He was the most capable man she knew. Surely he would save her. She had to believe, and to keep trying to escape her bonds.

~~~~~

Lord Geoffrey was irritated and dispirited. It was late afternoon when he slipped carefully from the hidden passages into his dressing room, and allowed Hurst to assist him with a change from clothing which was much the worse for wear from his explorations, for the last passages on this floor had been, it turned out, quite the filthiest of all of the areas that he had yet explored. Thank God that Hurst was one of the men provided by Setford, and knew of the mission.
~~~~~

The mission. The mission that was still incomplete. For he had found nothing but filth this afternoon. Exploring the hidden parts of the cellars was looking inevitable. Cleaner, but no happier, he went down to his study to await Lady Harriet's return, praying that her search had been more fruitful, and less filth-encrusted than his.

Settled into his favourite chair, with a warming glass of brandy in hand, he wondered what his days would be like, once this mission was finally done with. What would he do with his time, when the search was complete? *'What would he do, when he no longer had a reason to see Lady Harriet every day…?'*

He would wait until she was here to pull out the maps, for them to update any of the detail of the passages they had explored today. For now, he would simply rest, and try to improve his mood.

He took down the beautiful old swords from the wall, and ran his fingers along the blade. It was now not only clean and polished, but sharp, as it should be. The balance was wonderful, and, had he not been waiting for Lady Harriet, he would have been tempted to take the blades straight to the drawing room which he had cleared of furniture to use as a *salle*. A little sword work always cleared his thoughts of any frustration – weapons required a clear and focused mind.

An hour later, he began to be concerned. Surely she should have returned by now? Even if she had found another unmapped section, surely it would not have taken this long? Generally, she and Miss Carpenter departed by dusk at the latest, and it was past that hour now. The darkness was closing in.

What if something had happened to her? He would never forgive himself should she be hurt. It was one thing to talk of the risk involved in this mission, and to speak of accepting it – it was quite another to meet that danger head on.

In that instant, he saw his own feelings for her clearly. No matter how much he might have been denying it, he did care for her, with an intensity that was almost frightening. The thought of any harm coming to her was like a blade to his heart. How could he have allowed her to place herself at risk? How could he have been so selfish, wanting her company and the success of his mission above her safety?

At that moment, there was a tap on his door. He breathed a sigh of relief – but his relief was short-lived. The door opened to admit Miss Carpenter and Mr Featherstonehaugh – who looked surprised, and then concerned, when it became apparent that Lady Harriet was not in the room.

"She hasn't returned." Lord Geoffrey broke the silence.

"What shall we do?" Miss Carpenter's voice was soft, and she twisted her hands together as she spoke.

"I am going to look for her. Miss Carpenter, please get Walters to take a message to Pendholm Hall – tell them that I have invited you, and Lady Harriet to stay for dinner. Let us not concern her family unduly. Should I not return by the time dinner is called, please, eat, and assure the staff that I am simply busy."

He strode out the door, and, seeing Peterson on duty in the hallway, called him to follow.

It was only when Peterson looked enquiringly at the sword in his hand that he realised he still held it. Well and good then. A weapon in hand was not a bad thing, should there be trouble.

They began on the top floor, searching through each room, then moving into the hidden passages.

Some hours later, they had covered every inch of the place twice over, and found nothing. Outside the walls, dinner had come and gone.

The candle in their lantern was burnt down to a nub, casting little effective light, and Lord Geoffrey had reached a state of internal turmoil unlike anything he had ever felt before. The fear of losing Lady Harriet forever ate at him. Not knowing where she was, or what she might be suffering was torture of the worst kind.

He slumped back against the passage wall, close against the blank wall where it simply ended. Peterson lifted the lantern, to better see Lord Geoffrey's face, and opened his mouth to speak. Lord Geoffrey's hand whipped out to arrest the motion of the lantern.

"I thought so! Look, Peterson – just there, caught at the edge of that piece of wall."

Peterson peered at the spot Lord Geoffrey pointed to, at first seeing nothing. Then he reached out a careful hand, and touched the dark gold hair that had glinted in the lantern light. He tugged on it gently, but it seemed trapped – trapped between the blank wall and the side wall that Lord Geoffrey leant on.

"Her hair!" Lord Geoffrey's voice was rough with emotion. "But… how is it trapped? What is it caught on?"

"I think, my Lord, that this wall is not a wall. It must be another door, for the hair appears to go into the crack along its edge…"

Without a word, Lord Geoffrey pushed away from the wall and began to push and prod at every part of the surrounding surfaces.

Chapter Twelve

Lady Harriet had worn her wrists and ankles raw, but had not succeeded in loosening the ropes enough to slip out of them.

The light was fading from the tiny window, and, with full darkness, she knew that it would not be long before they came for her. But unless she could somehow escape the ropes, there was nothing she could do but pray that Lord Geoffrey found her, before she was beyond his reach forever. She wished, most fervently, that she had, at every opportunity, thrown herself into his arms, propriety be damned.

She remembered that one kiss, and wished for more. If she was never to see him again, she wished for more to remember. She had known, for more than a year now, that he was the man for her. These last few months had simply deepened that feeling, deepened her love for him. Did he realise? Did he know how much she felt for him? Did he care for her in return? Or were those momentary flashes of desire she had seen in his eyes only that – desire, not anything deeper?

Her thoughts were interrupted eventually, long after the window had gone dark, by the sound that she had been anticipating with dread. The sound of feet upon the hidden stairs. As the door opened, she abandoned the last of her hope. It was too late. Lord Geoffrey could not save her now, they were here to take her away, to a life too horrible to contemplate.

"Had a comfortable afternoon, have you mileddy?" Ashley, the footman, smiled at her as he spoke. It was not a pleasant smile.

"Let's get movin Ash, the quicker she's off and gone, the happier I'll be." Jobs stepped towards her, then paused. "How's we gonna carry her Ash? Them stairs is narrow and steep. If'n she wriggles too much, we could all end up at the bottom with broken bones."

"Carefully – we's carryin her carefully. We wants to protect our investment here, doesn't we? And you, mileddy, you'll a be keeping still for us, won't ye? Cause I'm thinkin ye've no more wish than us to fall, have ye?"

Lady Harriet shook her head. She most definitely didn't want to fall – alive and unhurt, there might still be a chance to escape – injured there would be none.

"Right then. I'll get her by the legs, and you be liftin under her arms. I'll go down them steps first, backwards and slow, and you'll keep pace wiv me, wiv her between us."

Ashley bent to lift her legs. Jobs looked at the door to the stairs uncertainly, then shrugged and shoved his hands under her upper body, hindered by her hands tied behind her.

She flinched at the feel of their uncaring hands on her, but did not fight. She chose, instead, to be as limp and heavy as possible. With two older brothers, she had learnt, long ago, that limp and heavy was much harder to lift and carry than wriggling and screaming.

The men grunted and hauled her up awkwardly, making so much noise that she did not, at first, notice any other sound. But she did notice something else. The air in the room had moved, stirred like a light breeze across her face, drifting a fine tendril of her hair into her eyes. She gave no sign of anything having changed, but inwardly she prayed. *'Please, let that touch of moving air mean what I think it might.'*

And then she heard it – definitely a sound. A sound she was deliriously happy to hear – the sound of the other door moving, ever so slowly. Let it be him, let it be Lord Geoffrey come to save her. The men started to cart her towards the door to the stairs, and for a moment she thought that she must have been mistaken.

~~~~~

Lord Geoffrey was ready to give up poking about and simply batter at the door, when his fingers found an odd bump, low down on the wall. A bit of pushing at it, and the wall popped open, just a crack, releasing a gentle puff of air that sent Lady Harriet's golden hair drifting to the floor.

"Finally!"

He pulled it open, and stepped through into another dark and empty passage. A short passage. With no visible exit.
~~~~~

Geoffrey groaned aloud, then began the process all over again. There had to be another way out. She had come in here, so she had to have gone out of here. He just had to find it. The walls were rougher here – more possible bumps and lumps to push and prod at. He worked along the passage on one side, whilst Peterson took the other. Just as they reached the apparent end of the short length of passage, he stopped, and froze in place, touching Peterson to make him stop too.

There was a sound, he was sure of it. From the other side of the wall. Creeping forward, he pressed his ear to the rough plaster and listened. Men's voices. Two, he thought. He couldn't make out what they said. Then a thump and a bump, as if they were moving something heavy about, and bumped into a chair or similar, then a muttered curse – he might not be able to hear the exact words, but the tone and emotion in it were clear enough.

As he pressed harder against the wall, desperate to hear more, his fingers caught on a simple latch. He lifted it, and the door shifted gently. The disturbed air carried a scent to him from within the space on the other side of the door. A scent he would recognise anywhere. Lady Harriet's perfume, that unique mix of rose, daphne and lemon. He closed his eyes, as much from horror as relief.

She was here – but she was in the hands of the traitors – was she hurt? Why was she silent? He could not imagine Lady Harriet going anywhere quietly, if it was against her will. He eased the door open a little, and peered into the room. Ashley and Jobs were struggling to lift a completely limp Lady Harriet, moving awkwardly towards a door on the other side of the small room.

His fear for her drove him to immediate action. He could not, as much as he wished it, simply drive his sword through Jobs' back, even though it was presented nicely before him – for the sword could just as easily penetrate the man and harm Harriet, limp in his arms, as well. He leapt forward and drove the hilt of the sword towards Jobs head, hoping to knock him out with one blow.

But as the blow landed, Jobs staggered under Lady Harriet's weight, and what should have been a solid collision with the man's head became a glancing blow instead. Jobs dropped her and spun, roaring in anger. Ashley, after one look at Lord Geoffrey, sword in hand and eyes wild, with Peterson behind him, somehow hauled Lady Harriet up and over his shoulder, then staggered to the stairs. For one second, before Jobs rushed him, fists windmilling in panicked attack, Lord Geoffrey found himself looking straight into Harriet's beseeching eyes.

Then she was gone, and he heard a bolt shot into place on the other side of the door, as Ashley carried her away. Desperation drove him. He would not lose her now! He would not let her down – that look had told him she believed in him – that she had the utmost faith in his ability to save her. To her, as always, he was a hero. Well – it was time he lived up to that then, though he had never sought it.

Then all thought disappeared, as battle reflexes honed at war cut in. He became a coldly focused fighting machine. A minute or two later, Jobs found himself flat on the floor, Lord Geoffrey's sword at his throat, as Peterson used some of the remaining scatter of old rope on the floor to bind him tightly.

"Where is he taking her?"

The sword still hovered at Jobs' throat, and Lord Geoffrey's voice made it clear that anything but the truth would result in pain or death. Jobs gulped, flinching as the movement of his throat caused the sword point to break his skin. Stammering from fear, he spoke, with a last spark of defiance.

"You'll be too late. He'll have her out and away afore ye can get down t'ground. Once she's in the cart, ye'll nivver see her agin."

Lord Geoffrey looked at Peterson, and they reached a silent agreement. Geoffrey ran to the now bolted door that Ashley had carried Harriet through, and began to batter it, using anything to hand. The bolt might not break – but the wood was old – batter it enough, and surely it would splinter.

Peterson spun and ran back the way they had come, through the hidden passages and out into the main part of the house. He flung himself down the stairs, yelling to Walters, who was stationed in the foyer, to get Hurst and follow, then charged out into the night. Where was the nearest lane to the estate? Where might a cart be hidden?

Meanwhile, the door had finally shattered under Lord Geoffrey's onslaught. Geoffrey slid down the narrow stairs, perilously close to falling, uncaring of his own safety in the desperate need to get to Harriet in time. Unregarded, in the room above, Jobs muttered pathetically about being abandoned, bound hand and foot. He was quite unaware of the appropriateness of him being left exactly as he had left Lady Harriet all day. He did, however, realise after a while that, unless he could escape now, he was dead – for he would surely hang for treason. He began to struggle against the ropes.

Reaching the ground floor, Lord Geoffrey sprinted through the servants' corridor. Shoving a startled maid aside, he charged out the door towards the stables, sword still in hand, silver in the moonlight. Skidding to a halt, he looked around. Where had Ashley gone with her?

Then he saw it – a moment's glint of moonlight on the gold of her hair. Near the edge of the trees, across the wide lawn. He had to be heading for the rutted lane that led to the old shepherd's cottage.

Geoffrey ran, ran as he had never run before in his life, glad that he heard Peterson's footsteps on the gravel behind him, before he hit the smooth grass of the lawn. In that instant, he blessed his gardeners – they would all be getting an increase in their wages, for the immaculate lawn made it easier to run. And he, a fit, large man, trained to fight, could run considerably faster than an older, somewhat unfit footman carrying a full grown woman.

He was gaining on them, but they were still ahead, and nearly at the small stone wall that marked his boundary. When Ashley reached the stile over the wall, another man leapt up onto it from the other side, reaching for Harriet.

"No! no, no, no, no!" The words were muttered, for all his breath was spent on running. But his heart's agony was in every one of them. As other hands lifted Harriet away, Lord Geoffrey swung his sword at Ashley's lower leg, waiting only a second to see him fall screaming, before leaving him for Peterson to deal with. He vaulted the stile and launched himself onto the back of the cart as it lurched into motion in response to the driver's desperate whipping of the horses.

He paused a second to touch a finger to Harriet's face, where she lay tumbled in the bed of the cart, and realised, as he did, that the driver had thought the shudder of the cart as he landed on it to be simply part of the violent lurch into motion. The man didn't know he was there!

Moving with infinite care, he felt his way down Harriet's arm and used the sword edge to cut the ropes that bound her. She bit down on the gag at the pain of returning circulation, but made no sound. He eased down to trace her leg to her ankles, silently wishing he was doing so in any circumstances but these, and sliced the ropes from her ankles too. As he did so, she was already pulling the gag from her mouth.

He crept up past her, pausing only long enough to press a kiss to her lips, and edged towards the front of the cart. He felt, rather than heard, Harriet easing her way after him. He turned to look at her, and her green eyes sparkled in the moonlight. She motioned towards the man, then to Geoffrey. Then she pointed at herself, and mimed her hands holding reins and driving.

His heart bursting with love and pride, he nodded once, and turned back to his task. She edged to one side, close against him, but not enough to prevent his movement. He tapped her hand three times, and launched himself. His arm went around the driver's throat, cutting off his air, and the sword came around to hang before the man's face, the threat obvious.

The driver squirmed desperately, the ribbons falling unregarded from his fingers, then froze in place when he saw the sword.

As he dropped the ribbons, Harriet launched herself from the back of the cart onto the seat, snatching the falling ribbons of leather from the air, a fraction of a second before they fell into the gap between cart and horses.

She teetered a moment on the brink of falling herself, and Geoffrey felt his heart stop in his chest, then she grabbed the seat with one hand and hauled herself back, already beginning to bring the racing horses under control. She was, it seemed, as good at driving them as riding them.

"That thrice damned bastard's name is Nobby. He had a deal with them, to sell me to a house of pleasure, and split the profits. I'd happily see you skewer him now, but I suspect we'd better turn him over to the law."

Her voice was a little shaky, but not, he realised from fear. It was anger he heard, pure and simple. She was, quite simply, magnificent.

"Oh. That wasn't very ladylike language was it? I am sorry, but in this case, I rather think I'm entitled to swear."

He laughed, a shaky, almost hysterical edge to it.

"I believe you're right."

He kept the sword to Nobby's throat, while Harriet brought the straining horses back to a walk, then turned them carefully in a wider bit of the lane, before driving them back toward Witherwood Chase at a smart clip.

~~~~~
~~~~~

By the time they reached the stile again, Peterson had bound the bleeding Ashley, and Walters and Hurst were ready with ropes to bind Nobby. They hauled the screaming Ashley on to the back of the cart, and Harriet drove them all back around through the gates and up the drive to the stables.

Once the horses were held by the grooms, Lord Geoffrey slipped from the seat, supervising the traitors' removal from the cart, and the field dressing of Ashley's wound. He didn't want the man dying on him from an infection, before he'd had time to tell him where the papers were. Satisfied that things were under control, he turned back to the cart.

Lady Harriet was simply sitting there, staring ahead. She was, he realised, shaking, quivering like a leaf in the wind. He knew this reaction – he had seen it after battles, when the aftershock of action set in. Gently, he stepped up as close to the cart as he could, and, reaching out, slid her into his arms and lifted her down. She came willingly, sliding her arms around his neck, and burying her face against his shoulder. He thought she whispered something, but it was so faint he wasn't sure. It had sounded suspiciously like *'My hero'*.

He carried her into the house.

Chapter Thirteen

Lord Geoffrey settled Lady Harriet onto a chaise in the parlour, rang for tea, and brandy, and sat quietly beside her. She said nothing, but simply reached out and twined her fingers with his.

When the maid brought the tea and brandy, it was obvious that the staff were agog to know what was happening. They would have to wait. He shooed the maid out and poured a cup of tea, adding a generous drop of brandy. Harriet accepted it gratefully, and sipped.

Peterson knocked and entered when bidden, reporting that the traitors were bound and locked up in a secure room in the stables, with Walters guarding them. Lord Geoffrey nodded his thanks. Peterson turned to go, when Lady Harriet spoke.

"Please stay, Peterson. For you should hear what I have to tell, given your part in this mission."

Peterson hesitated, and, at Lord Geoffrey's confirmatory nod, stepped back into the room.

Her voice hesitant at first, then growing stronger as she spoke, and the brandy took effect, Lady Harriet described the events of the day. When she spoke of the box that she had seen, just before Ashley and Jobs had bound and gagged her, Lord Geoffrey sprang to his feet, pacing about the room. Could it really be over? Was that box the end to this mission? But where had they taken it? He broke in on her tale.

"Was there anything in what they said to indicate where they took the box?" She stared at him a moment, face blank, and he castigated himself for behaving in such an inconsiderate way - here he was, expecting her to have taken detailed note of what the men were saying, when she had just been roughly set upon, bound, gagged and threatened!

"I am so sorry! That is completely unreasonable of me to ask."

Lady Harriet looked up at him and smiled. His heart turned over at what he saw in her eyes.

"Ah, but I did listen to them. I was so utterly, blazingly angry, it hadn't yet occurred to me to be truly afraid. That came later. Just before they left the room, Ashley said something about taking it down to *'the deep'* and putting it with *'the other'*. It was just a single comment, before they left me there. They had put the box in a basket of dirty linens and covered it up. Probably so that they could take it down into the cellars somewhere, and be thought to be just adding a basket to the laundry pile. But beyond down in the cellars, which seems logical, I've no idea where *'the deep'* might be."

Frustration laced her voice. They might have the conspirators, but they didn't yet have the evidence.

Lord Geoffrey thought a moment, pacing about the room, then spun back towards her.

"Wait – they spoke of 'another' something?"

"Yes – they definitely were going to put the box with *'the other'*."

"But that's wonderful! Forgive me, I know that sounds terrible of me, but had today's events not happened, we would never have known of this second thing that is hidden. If we had found this box when they were not there, we would most certainly have believed that we had found all that there was to find."

Lord Geoffrey fell to his knees beside her, and pulled her into his arms, pressing a kiss to her lips as he did so. She clung to him, a little puzzled but delighted by his actions. Peterson met her eyes over Lord Geoffrey's shoulder and smiled. Lord Geoffrey pulled back and gazed at her.

"Oh Harriet, you are truly wonderful! Whilst I would never wish for you to have suffered what you have today, I am beyond grateful for what you have discovered. Your courage and resourcefulness never cease to amaze me. When any society miss might be expected to have fainted dead away, you were alert enough to listen and take note. And then on the cart! You are magnificent, magnificent!"

He had spoken her name! Without the 'Lady' in front of it! Her heart suddenly beat harder, the intimacy of her unadorned name on his lips leaving her even more flushed than the kiss.

Peterson cleared his throat, whilst feigning great interest in a book which had been left lying on a side table.

Lord Geoffrey, who had, for those moments, completely forgotten Peterson's presence, dropped Harriet's hands and leapt to his feet, a flush of embarrassment on his face.

"Ah, Peterson, it seems that we will need to interrogate our prisoners. I am sure that one of them can be convinced to tell us where the box is hidden. That would be considerably quicker than searching every hidden part of the cellars that the maps show, and probably parts that exist, but aren't on the maps."

Lord Geoffrey shuddered internally, even as he spoke. He hated interrogations. A good clean fight was one thing, but the process of drawing information forth was a dirty thing. Gerry had always been the one amongst the Hounds who dealt with that – expertly and efficiently. They were all beyond grateful that he had done that dirty work for them. Tonight, Geoffrey would have to deal with it himself.

"Yes, my Lord, I will arrange that – tonight – the less time they have to think about it, the more likely they are to tell us. Will you wish to be present?"

Lord Geoffrey took a deep steadying breath.

"Yes, it is my duty to do so."

Peterson nodded, having expected nothing less.

"And, my Lord, shall I arrange for Lady Harriet and Miss Carpenter to be conveyed home? And what message do you wish delivered to Viscount Pendholm to explain all of this?"

Harriet paled. The thought of explaining all of this to her brother and mother did not appeal at all.

They were reasonable people, and Charlton, she knew, had dealt with traitors before, but neither of them would be happy about her involvement in this mission, especially when they heard the details of today's events. But hear they would, for it was now past any reasonable time for her to be returning, even after a supposed dinner.

"I think that, before we consider returning Lady Harriet to her home, we must first call for some ointment for her poor wrists and ankles, which are, I now see, worn quite raw from her struggles. I do apologise, Lady Harriet, for not having that attended to sooner. Also, I suspect that some food would not go amiss, as you have had nothing since breaking your fast this morning."

Harriet looked positively enthusiastic at the suggestion of food. It was, at least in part, because that would delay facing her family, but the embarrassingly loud growl of her stomach was a pointed reminder of her actual need to eat.

"Whilst those matters are addressed, let us deal with our prisoners. Once that is done, I will personally escort Lady Harriet and Miss Carpenter to Pendholm Hall."

Harriet met his eyes, her gratitude and relief showing clearly.

"Thank you, Lord Geoffrey, your escort will be most appreciated."

<div align="center">~~~~~</div>

The three prisoners, when asked questions separately, demonstrated rather different reactions.

Nobby refused to say anything, knowing full well that there was enough wrongdoing in his past to deliver him to the hangman's noose no matter what he said now. Lord Geoffrey let him be – for he had, as far as they could tell, no knowledge of what had gone on inside the house.

Ashley and Jobs were another matter. Threats of immediate violence had little effect on Ashley, but Jobs was quickly persuaded that cooperation might, perhaps, save him from the hangman's noose. Compared to death, transportation seemed a far better option. Lord Geoffrey gave his word that, if Jobs provided them a guide to the location of the hidden box, he would do his best to ensure that transportation was the sentence. But only once they had recovered the box – if Jobs gave them falsehoods, he would make certain the sentence was death.

"Jus' one other thing, milord. If'n I tells ye, don' ye be putting me back near Ash. If'n he knows I've ratted him out, I'm a goner for sure."

"That can be arranged. Now speak."

Peterson took careful notes as Jobs described the path to the secret doors in the cellars, and the exact location of the hidden boxes. Lord Geoffrey was startled to hear that below the cellars, there was not only a priesthole, dating back to the time of Cromwell, but below even that, a secret chapel with an ancient altar. The boxes were, sacrilegiously, it seemed, hidden in a cavity within the altar itself. Finally, when Lord Geoffrey was satisfied that they had all of the information needed to recover the boxes, Jobs was locked away separately, still securely bound.

But confirming the truth of his words would need to wait for the morning. For now, he must face Lady Harriet's family, and admit to the terrible danger he had placed her in, by allowing her to assist him. He would understand should they forbid him from ever seeing her again. At least his mind would. His heart was not so sanguine about that possibility. The ache in his chest at the very thought suggested that such a possibility would leave him empty forever.

~~~~~

Harriet perched on the edge of the carriage seat, desperately wishing that she could lean against Lord Geoffrey's temptingly close shoulder. But fear of the coming conversation kept her from moving. Miss Carpenter had exclaimed over her poor wrists and ankles, and tutted about the battered state of her dress, but said nothing further. Harriet knew that she would honour their agreement and support her.

When they alighted before Pendholm Hall, Lord Geoffrey graciously offered her his arm, and led her inside. The warmth of the strong muscle beneath her hand reached her, even through the layers of his shirt and coat, making her feel safe and protected somehow, as she had felt in his arms when he had lifted her down from the cart.

Lord Geoffrey, at that moment, was feeling quite as nervous as she was, if not more so, although he strove to keep his manner steady and calm, for her. Her scent wrapped about him, bringing, as it always did, that sense of safety and care. They would manage this conversation, together.
~~~~~

When they were admitted to the house, they were shown to Lady Sylvia's private parlour. As was their habit, Charlton and his mother had settled for a late evening coze, to talk through the events of their day. Lady Odette had already retired, happy to allow Charlton this time with his mother, knowing that he would not stay away from her long.

Charlton took one look at Lord Geoffrey's face, and his sister's dirtied and torn morning dress, and leapt to his feet. Miss Carpenter followed them into the room, and the door closed behind her.

"What has happened?"

"Oh my poor child – your wrists – what has happened to you?"

Charlton's voice tangled with Lady Sylvia's as they both spoke at once.

"It is rather a long story, I am afraid, but it must be told now, despite the late hour." Lord Geoffrey sounded more nervous than Charlton had ever heard him. Geoff didn't do nervous – in all their years at war, he had always been cool and steady, no matter what happened. This would be most interesting.

"Do sit then, and I'll call for some tea." Lady Sylvia was as practical as ever. In that moment, Harriet thanked God for her mother's nature. They sat, Geoffrey and Harriet instinctively staying together, sinking gratefully onto a comfortable chaise. Miss Carpenter settled on a small chair in one corner of the room, and tried hard to be invisible.

A somewhat strained silence ensued.

Once a maid had delivered the tea, and left them with it, Charlton's patience failed him.

"Out with it Geoff – I can see that there is a lot to tell, so please get on with it – or... is it Harriet's story to tell?" He looked at Harriet, waiting. Harriet looked at Lord Geoffrey, and some unspoken communication passed between them, which Lady Sylvia observed with great interest, then Geoffrey spoke.

"I'll start at the beginning. Charlton, you know I've been working for Selford. Lady Sylvia, I'll repeat this part for your benefit. You already know that I received ownership of Witherwood Chase as reward for services to the crown during last year. What you don't know, but Charlton is at least a little aware of, is that along with the property, I received a mission. The previous owner of Witherwood Chase was part of a treasonous plot. When it was discovered, he was dispossessed of all his belongings and incarcerated with many of his conspirators. But not, Setford suspected, all of them. So the price of me receiving the property was to ferret out any evidence still hidden there, and the remaining conspirators."

He paused for a sip of tea, feeling a little better now that he had begun.

"Hence my obsessive poking into every corner of the house, and taking inventory of everything I found. Which, I must say, has proved a capital idea. One which is set to make me a remarkably wealthy man, when all of those ugly paintings are sold. When Lady Harriet volunteered..."

At this description, Charlton snorted, and Lady Sylvia smiled in amusement. Geoffrey fixed them with a baleful look.

"As I said, when Lady Harriet volunteered to assist, I was most grateful. For, whilst she and Miss Carpenter trailed around with Mr Featherstonehaugh, taking interminable notes about the obvious contents of the house, I was free to search for hidden things. Things which I conclusively failed to find."

"Ah," Charlton broke in, "which was when you sought our suggestions at Meltonbrook Chase, about ways in which hidden rooms or passages might be concealed, and how to find them."

"Correct. Shortly after that, accidentally, Lady Harriet stumbled, quite literally, on a secret door, and opened it. Only I was present at that moment. Inside the room revealed, we discovered detailed maps of the entire house, showing most of the secret passages and rooms as well. We initially kept it between ourselves, but then found ourselves forced to draw Miss Carpenter and Mr Featherstonehaugh into our confidence to some degree."

At mention of her name, Miss Carpenter squirmed uncomfortably on her chair. So much for not being noticed....

"The last few weeks we have searched, usually separately, through every hidden passage we could. And found nothing but more dust and mouse droppings. This morning, we moved into the last two sections of the passages, except for the cellars. I admit, I was not hopeful, and searching the cellars, with access through the servants' areas was not a task I looked forward to."

Lady Sylvia nodded, listening to Lord Geoffrey, but watching Harriet's face.

"By late afternoon, I had finished searching my allocated section of the passages, with no better luck than on any previous day. I waited in my study for Lady Harriet's return. But today, she did not appear at the expected time. I waited, thinking that perhaps she had found some extra passages, and it was taking longer. But then I realised that it was far too late. I sent you that message – I do wholeheartedly apologise for the subterfuge – so as not to worry you unnecessarily, and set out to search for her."

Lady Sylvia had gone very pale, and was looking, again, at Harriet, and her bandaged wrists. Geoffrey continued, telling the tale of his frustrated and increasingly fearful search, the discovery of Harriet's hair trapped in the passage, and his reaching the room where she was held. When he spoke of noticing the hair and thus finding the door, Harriet gazed at him with open adoration.

At that point, Harriet spoke up, taking over the telling of the tale, describing her day, how she had stumbled upon the secret doors, and walked in on the conspirators, only to be captured and bound. When she spoke of the plans they had made for her, Charlton's face went hard as stone. When she reached the point in the story where Geoffrey had arrived at the room, he joined her in the telling of the rest, their voices interweaving as they shifted from one part to the next, instinctively finishing each other's sentences until the tale was complete.

Lord Geoffrey spoke of her heroic capture of the ribbons and controlling the horses, Harriet spoke of Lord Geoffrey's heroic disabling of Ashley, his leap to the cart, and the capture of Nobby.

To Charlton and Lady Sylvia, watching them, it was very obvious that the bond between them was extraordinary, and that something remarkable had been forged that day, beyond the achievement of capturing the villains. Lady Sylvia wondered if Harriet and Geoffrey had admitted their feelings to each other yet.

"So there you have it. A sordid and distressing tale. I can only most humbly beg your forgiveness for ever placing Lady Harriet in such danger. I will never forgive myself. At that moment when she teetered on the cart, I knew that my life would not be worth living if I had lost her. Now, to complete this damnable mission, all that remains is to go into the cellars tomorrow morning, and retrieve the hidden boxes, confirm that their contents are what Setford seeks, and allow him to carry off the conspirators and the papers."

"I insist on being the one to open that altar and remove the boxes. After all of this, I think I'm entitled to that." Harriet's voice was strong, and her bright cheerful manner was returning, even after all the shocks of the day.

Geoffrey looked at her a moment, then nodded.

"Charlton, would you do me the honour of being there as well? I would like another witness to this, one that Setford knows and trusts."

"Certainly, I wouldn't miss it!"

"You're not leaving me out of this either! After what my daughter has been through for those boxes, I want to see them with my own eyes."

Lord Geoffrey, seeing a glint in Lady Sylvia's eyes that was a rather clear echo of her daughter in a determined mood, inclined his head in acknowledgement. She smiled.

"Good, we are agreed then. We will bring Harriet to Witherwood Chase in the morning, and see this thing complete. And Lord Geoffrey – of course I forgive you – I am fully aware of how difficult it is to prevent my daughter from doing anything that she truly wishes to do. I do not blame you in the least. But I am overwhelmingly glad that you were there to save her – as you saved us all last year."

Lord Geoffrey flushed at Lady Sylvia's words.

"You are most gracious my Lady. I will look forward to your arrival on the morrow."

He turned to Lady Harriet, took her hand a moment, and bent to kiss it, before standing and bowing to the others, then took his leave.

~~~~

In the carriage, he allowed himself to relax, and discovered, to his chagrin, that he was shaking. He had been so afraid that they might blame him, might cast him from their house, that he might never see Harriet again.

The relief was overwhelming. He could not bear to never see her. He loved her, he wanted to…

What! What had he just thought? He rewound the thoughts and there it was. He loved her. It was a startling idea, yet it seemed utterly right.
~~~~

But... how did she really feel about him?   What if her affection really was just the infatuation he had always thought it? What would he do?

Chapter Fourteen

Harriet had barely slept, between the aching in her arms and legs from the long hours bound in awkward positions, and the exertion afterwards on the cart, and the feverish dreams of Lord Geoffrey's arms about her, and his lips on hers, all mixed in with more terrible dreams of being bound in the darkness.

She tried to sit patiently whilst her maid dressed the wounds on her wrists and ankles again, wincing a little at the pressure on the sensitive flesh, then found herself still ravenous after the exertions of the previous day. Lady Sylvia was happy to see that Harriet's appetite was undiminished by her adventures.

Once in the carriage, she fidgeted, anxious to see Lord Geoffrey again, desperate to finally see the papers that had brought them all so much trouble, and, at the same time, afraid of what would follow. The days ahead looked bleak and empty if she should no longer have an excuse to spend them in Lord Geoffrey's company.

She had thought, last night, when he had cared for her, held her, that she saw something in his eyes, in his manner, that she had longed for, this year past and more. In the grey morning light, she was no longer sure. Did he care for her, truly, or was it just her wishes making her see what wasn't there? If he did not care for her, what would she do? For she loved him. She had from almost the first time she had met him. That would not change. She had known that he was the man she wanted, been quite certain of her feelings from the start – but how would she live if he never returned her love, or even affection?

As Witherwood Chase came into sight, she pushed those thoughts aside – first, the cellars, and the boxes of papers.

They were shown into the study and Lord Geoffrey greeted them a little seriously, although his eyes locked with Harriet's the moment she stepped into the room. That moment seemed to last forever, and to be gone too fast. He dragged his eyes away, and, showing them to seats placed near the desk, he brought forth the maps of the house.

Peterson had been busy, and had marked, on the map of the cellars, the places described by Jobs. Once they were all clear on the path before them, Lord Geoffrey rose.

"Shall we get this over with?"

"By all means. I would like to see these papers that are so precious as to be, apparently, worth my life and more." Lady Harriet rose from her seat. Lord Geoffrey led her from the room, followed by the others. The servants were shocked at the procession that entered their domain, and scurried aside.

At the back of the root cellar, Peterson led them to a section where sacks of various vegetables hung on hooks, and larger barrels of potatoes and onions stood below. Once the barrels were shifted aside, a push and pull on two of the hooks at once caused the panel to open, exposing dark steps beyond, steep and uneven. Lantern in hand, he led them downwards.

The steps turned, and finally deposited them in a small room carved out of the earth. Nooks carved into the wall served as shelves, and a space for a narrow bed. A trickle of water fell from a small hole in the rocks to one side, no doubt fed from the rain water cisterns above, and pooled in an old earthenware bowl, before overflowing to trickle out again through a crack in one corner of the floor. It was well constructed as a place in which a man could hide for a long time, given a supply of food. Harriet shuddered at the thought of priests being forced to hide in such places, those many years ago.

Turning, they studied the space. Where was the secret entry to the chapel, which Jobs had described? Lord Geoffrey, eyes narrowed, strode forward and swept the mouldering blanket from the boards that covered the earth in the nook designed as a bed. Grasping the boards, he lifted, and revealed, not the beaten earth that was to be expected, but a small space and more stairs leading down into inky darkness.

Again, Peterson took the lead, checking the steps for safety, and holding the lantern, as best he might, to allow them to see where they stepped. Lord Geoffrey assisted Lady Harriet, and Charlton assisted Lady Sylvia, who grimaced a little at the smears of earth now decorating their clothes.

When they reached the bottom, they gasped in awe. Whoever had built this had spent much effort and care. They stood in a small chapel, the walls lined with stone, plastered and decorated with paintings – religious imagery in a style many centuries gone, the colours still beautiful, only lightly touched with mould in a few places. Small gems embedded in parts of the pictures glinted in the lantern light, and silver candlesticks shone in nooks and on either end of the plain altar.

The altar was built of stone and wood, carved with elegant simplicity. Harriet stepped forward, and walked around it, wondering exactly where it opened.

"On the end, my Lady. The two floral pieces to either side of the cross in the carving. According to Jobs, they must both be pressed at once, and the timber panel on the end will open. In these old altars, they made these cavities to store relics – often the bones of saints, I believe." Lord Geoffrey's voice was muted. This might be long unused, but they all felt the sense of the intended sanctity of the place.

Harriet, praying that no bones of a saint graced this altar, sharing their housing with sacrilegious boxes of traitorous information, did as instructed. The panel popped out as they had been told it would, and she lifted it aside. Reaching in, she pulled out two boxes – one that she had seen upstairs, one which was larger and heavier, and passed them to Peterson, who sat them on the single simple pew.

They looked so insignificant, yet, for what these contained, men had been willing to destroy her life. Charlton tested each box.

"Locked. As was to be expected. How do we plan to open them."

"I have no key, and Jobs didn't know of the key's location either, but…" Lord Geoffrey had turned towards Lady Harriet, with a hopeful expression. He smiled when he saw that she was already pulling a pin from her soft gold hair.

She pushed past her brother and sank down onto the pew.

"Peterson, the light, if you would."

Peterson brought the lantern close and both Charlton and Lady Sylvia watched in some astonishment as Lady Harriet carefully picked the locks on both boxes. With a satisfied expression, she replaced the pin in her hair and turned shining eyes to Lord Geoffrey.

"There my Lord. If you would open them now, we may at last see what all of this fuss has been for."

Lord Geoffrey was watching Lady Harriet with unfeigned admiration. He bowed elegantly to her, with a flourish worthy of Mr Featherstonehaugh, and stepped forward.

The boxes proved to contain, as Baron Setford had expected, a collection of papers detailing meetings, conspirators' names, plans, and other deeply damning evidence of treason. They also contained a few small bags of coinage, and of gemstones, which was not expected. In the larger box, a small ledger listed payments made – a source of information that would delight Setford and no doubt lead his men to many of those who had supported the plot, however peripherally.

Papers. So innocent looking, and yet enough to send many men to their deaths. Lady Harriet shuddered, and gently closed the lids.

"Let us be out of this place. That so many should have plotted against our country leaves me feeling sickened." No-one disagreed.

~~~~~

Urgent messages were sent, and, three days later, Baron Setford arrived. He brought a second carriage, with barred windows and armed men to guard it. The prisoners were handed over to his guards, and the carriage departed, taking them to their fate. Lord Geoffrey, true to his word, told Setford of his promise to Jobs, and the Baron agreed that, under the circumstances, he would most likely be able to get the man transported, rather than hung.

Late in the evening, Lord Geoffrey, Charlton and Baron Setford took their ease in Geoffrey's study. Brandy in their glasses, and the boxes resting on the desk in front of them, they went over the events of the last few days again, for Setford's benefit.

He listened intently as Lord Geoffrey told the tale, leaving nothing out. He examined the contents of the boxes, and nodded, pleased. This would leave no loose ends. This matter would finally be done, and he could now report it as such to the Prince Regent. He hefted the bags of coin and gems, his shrewd grey eyes considering. Then he turned, and dropped them into Lord Geoffrey's hands.
~~~~~

"Excellent work. How convenient that these boxes contained only the papers we sought, and all of the papers we sought. And, from your description, I am most impressed with young Lady Harriet. She would, I suspect, have the talent to make an excellent contribution to our work. I don't suppose you'd consider recruiting her?"

"No!"

"Definitely not!"

Charlton and Geoffrey spoke at once, both glaring at Setford, who laughed.

"That's what I thought you'd say. But you can't blame me for asking – it's not often we find a woman with courage, and useful skills like lock picking!"

"True. It's not a talent I was aware my sister had, until today."

Charlton looked chagrined at admitting this.

"Apparently," Lord Geoffrey contributed, "she learnt that skill as a child, to recover her prized possessions when your nasty piece of a brother had locked them away. I am not surprised that she has kept it secret. It's not exactly a socially approved 'suitable skill for a Lady'."

Charlton looked thoughtful, wondering just how it was that Geoffrey knew more about his sister than he did.

Setford finished his brandy and reached out to close the lids of the boxes.

"Please lock these away for tonight."

As Geoffrey did so, Setford continued.

"I'll be away tomorrow with these, and set things in motion. I will keep you apprised of the outcomes. But it may take a month before I have much news for you."

"In that case, let me invite you to partake of my hospitality again – the Hounds and their families intend to gather here for Eastertide, and we would be delighted if you would join us."

Setford stilled, and, for the first time ever, Geoffrey saw something in his pale grey eyes that looked alarmingly like uncertainty. Then he nodded, as if coming to a decision.

"I'd be delighted m'boy. Catching up with all of you at once will be a pleasure. But now, let's to our rest. I, at least, have a long day ahead of me tomorrow."

Chapter Fifteen

To Harriet, the week after they had descended into the hidden chapel, and recovered the evidence against the traitors, passed in an odd dream like way. The whole thing, after months of searching, and the drama of her almost abduction, seemed monumentally anticlimactic. Her abraded wrists and ankles healed, but her heart ached.

She wanted to see Lord Geoffrey, missed him dreadfully, in fact, after so long seeing him almost every day. She had hoped, at first, that he might come to visit her. He did not. Charlton told her that he had been very busy with Baron Setford, seeing off the prisoners and handing over the boxes. She supposed that was reasonable – but that did not make her heart ache any less.

Lord Geoffrey, once Setford was gone, found himself at a loose end, unable to settle to anything. The funds from the sale of the first batch of paintings had been deposited to his bank, and Raphael had sent him a quick letter, telling him so, and informing him of the astounding sum involved.

Mr Featherstonehaugh, who seemed equally a little out of sorts and lost, was working at finalising the inventory and packing of the next two shipments of goods to be sold. These would not be sent to Raphael until after Easter, for Raphael had also written to advise that he would be away again for some weeks. He neglected to mention why.

Which left Lord Geoffrey with absolutely nothing to do. Except think. About Lady Harriet, to be precise. All the time. He felt like a lovesick boy. He busied himself with simple things - visits to the tenant farmers, and meetings with each and every remaining member of his staff. He wanted them to know that they were not under suspicion, that he valued their work.

Universally, they greeted that news with relief, and a cautious warming of their attitude to him. Mrs Chester even went so far as to confide that 'she'd never held with them strange types the old master went about with'. Whilst it all needed to be done, none of it really distracted him. Thoughts of Lady Harriet were ever present in the back of his mind. He wanted to see her. Truth be told, he wanted much more than to just see her. He wanted to hold her, to kiss her, to be near her every day.

But the only way he could do that would be to... he shied away from the thought. He sent no message, for he had no idea what he could say. And the longer he was away from her, the more doubts he felt. What if she hated him for having endangered her, now that she'd had time to recover and think about it? If he didn't see her, there was still hope.

So it went for a week or more, until an invitation arrived.

Lady Sylvia would be delighted if he would join them for dinner on the morrow. His heart leapt, with hope and fear at once. He would see her. But what if she did not wish to see him? Still, cursing himself for having been a coward, when that had never been his way, he accepted the invitation. The hours until that dinner lasted longer than any other day of his life.

~~~~~

Lady Sylvia had watched her daughter with some concern. Where was her bright, volatile child? This moody drifting girl was not her Harriet! How had it come to a point where Harriet, who had determinedly pursued Lord Geoffrey's company at any opportunity, for over a year now, was limply fretting rather than acting?

In the end, with that sense of mischief which was part of her (and which she had passed on to Harriet), she could not resist interfering, just a little. She invited Lord Geoffrey to dinner, only informing Harriet, Charlton and Odette after she had sent the invitation.

Harriet's face lit up at her words, then clouded with some fretting concern. Charlton watched the emotions chase across Harriet's face, raised an enquiring eyebrow at his mother, then smiled.

"An excellent idea mother."

Lady Odette happily agreed.
~~~~~

Odette was still adjusting to becoming mistress of a large household, and was more comfortable deferring to Lady Sylvia's judgement as yet.

Lady Sylvia went on her way to discuss menus with Cook, and Harriet, suspecting that Charlton would ask her about her expression, developed a sudden desire to go and ride Moonbeam, as she had been rather shamefully neglecting the mare of late. Charlton wisely let her go – Harriet would work out whatever was worrying her, all in good time.

~~~~~

When John led out Moonbeam for her, Harriet smiled and thanked him as he boosted her into the saddle.

"I know you'll follow me John, but please, give me at least the illusion of being alone. I need some time to think."

The groom bowed in acknowledgement.

"As you wish, my Lady."

The mare was fresh, and keen to run, so Harriet let her do so, enjoying the feel of the wind on her face, and the scent of the first spring grass as it was crushed beneath Moonbeam's hooves. When they reached the river's edge, she slowed the mare to a walk for a while, until she reached her favourite spot.

Slipping down, she tethered Moonbeam and settled on the large fallen log that afforded a view to the bend of the river. She had told the truth when she said she needed to think.
~~~~~

This evening, she would see Lord Geoffrey again. What would she do? How would he react?

She was quite certain that, as soon as she saw him, she would have the completely inappropriate urge to throw herself into his arms. Which she could not allow herself to do. For, before she completely embarrassed herself, she needed some indication of his feelings. Did he truly care for her? Or was she deluding herself. And how was she to discover the truth?

The afternoon flowed away with the river, and she was no closer to having answers to those questions. Soon, she would need to return, to dress for dinner, and prepare for the moment when he walked into the room. Just a few minutes more. As she stared into the distance, a sound came to her – quiet at first, then getting louder. Hoofbeats.

~~~~~

Lord Geoffrey could no longer stand the slow creep of the minutes. He had to do something to fill the hours before the dinner at Pendholm Hall. He stared out of the window at the gardens, where the approach of spring was bringing new leaves and the first buds of flowers, and decided to ride.

He could take Rajah out for a good gallop, take a turn past the furthest tenant farmers' cottages, and then make his way to the lower ford, cross, and go to Pendholm Hall along their side of the river. He was sure that Lady Sylvia would forgive his appearing for dinner in riding clothes rather than full evening attire. Decided, he called for Hurst, and went to dress.
~~~~~

Half an hour later, he sped across the fields, feeling freer than he had in months.

The tenant farmers were glad to see him, and he noted with pleasure that they, and their families, looked in much better health than they had when he first came to Witherwood Chase. Good shelter and enough food through the winter had made a difference. A difference that was sure to also result in better crops this summer, and in the years to follow.

The river was high with the last of the snow melt from the hills, but the ford was still easily passable. He slowed Rajah and simply soaked in the beauty of his surroundings, deeply appreciative of land not touched by war. Even after more than a year back in England, he could not forget the destruction of the land that the war had wrought, in France, and in Spain.

Coming closer to Pendholm Hall, he rounded a corner of the path and saw ahead of him a horse standing quietly, and beyond it a person, perched on a fallen log. Immediately he recognised the horse as Moonbeam, and the dappled sunlight glinting off Lady Harriet's hair made her identity unmistakable.

His mind froze. Rajah continued along the path at a steady walk, unconcerned with the turmoil of his master's mind.

What would he do? He could not give in to his first impulse, which was to rush to her, fling himself from the horse and gather her into his arms. What if she did not wish him to do so? What if she bitterly resented the danger that he had placed her in? He had no answers. Rajah reached the small clearing, and stopped, whickering a greeting to Moonbeam as he did so.

Lady Harriet turned, her green eyes wide, and a hesitant smile touched her face.

He drank in the sight of her.

Well, not hate then, if she was smiling – that was good.

Time seemed to slow, and he slid from the horse, his eyes never leaving hers. They each stepped forward, until they stood mere inches apart, neither sure what to say, how to breach the gap that had somehow appeared between them.

His voice came out a whisper.

"Harriet…"

She watched his storm grey eyes, and saw the message in them, that he struggled for words to express. She sighed, and a tightness left her posture, which she had not even realised was there.

Of its own accord, her hand reached for him, as surely as her words.

"Geoffrey… I…."

He took her hand, pulling her into his arms, and swept her words away with his lips, kissing her as he had so often dreamed of doing, as she wrapped her arms around his neck and pressed herself to him. Long minutes later, they pulled away from each other a little, still unsure of what to say, but each certain of their feelings. Keeping her fingers twined in his, Geoffrey took a deep steadying breath.

Now was the time to speak, no matter how much the words were hard to find.

"Harriet… I… I have missed you abominably this past week. Can you forgive me for not calling? I am ashamed to admit that I was afraid – afraid that you would not wish to see me, that you might hate me for having put you in such danger."

Harriet put her finger to his lips, arresting his words.

"Never think such a thing! I could never hate you. You have always been a hero to me, and the events of last week have only made that more so."

He lifted her hand, and pressed a kiss to her fingers.

"Then… if you cannot hate me, can I dare to hope that you might be able to love me? For I have discovered that I love you, beyond any sense or reason. When I saw you come so close to falling from that cart, I knew that I could never live without you. Harriet, my wonderful brave and clever Harriet, will you marry me?"

His breathing stopped, and he stood, utterly still, waiting for her response. She tipped her head to one side, and her green eyes sparkled, then she laughed with delight.

"Yes, oh yes, of course I will marry you. How could you think otherwise? I have loved you from the moment I saw you!"

He swept her into his arms again, spinning her around, her feet in the air, as she laughed with joy. When he set her feet to the ground again, she clung to him, dizzy with happiness.

For some time they simply stood that way, safe in each other's' arms, until the lengthening shadows reminded them that it was time to go.

Harriet, in that moment, suddenly realised that John must have seen, from a distance, the whole thing. And he had done nothing. How wonderful! She must thank him later.

Geoffrey boosted her onto Moonbeam, then mounted Rajah, and they set off along the path to Pendholm Hall.

"As soon as we arrive, I shall speak to Charlton. Er, how do you think he will react? Will he approve? Will your mother approve?"

Harriet looked at him like he was quite mad.

"Of course they will approve. And, if they seem to have any doubts, I will convince them."

This was the Harriet he loved – strong minded, determined, bright and beautiful.

~~~~~

Charlton laughed at the worried look on Geoffrey's face.

"Of course I approve! I shall be proud to call you brother-in-law, as well as brother-in-arms. I never thought to see this day, yet I should have known. My sister has always had a knack for getting what she wants – and she made no bones about wanting you."

Geoffrey's face lit with a grin to match Charlton's.

"I thought that we might have the wedding at Witherwood Chase, at Easter, when everyone will be here. That's just more than the necessary month needed for the banns. And I doubt Harriet wants to wait longer, any more than I do."
~~~~~

Geoffrey actually blushed as he spoke, and Charlton laughed again, clapping him on the shoulder.

"Come then, let's go and tell mother the news. I suspect if we take any longer to come out of this room, Harriet will come bursting in, ready to force me to agree!"

Lady Sylvia embraced Geoffrey, smiling with tears in her eyes.

"At first I was not so sure that you were right for her, you know. But the more I saw you with her, the more right it seemed. I cannot imagine a better man for my wild child of a daughter!"

At that moment, Harriet burst into the room, Charlton captured her before she had taken more than two steps, and spun her around, laughing at her expression.

"Harriet, I approve, and so does mother. You've no need to demand our agreement."

She stopped, and had the grace to flush, before looking up defiantly and reaching for Geoffrey's hand.

Epilogue

Their Easter gathering was full of life and happiness, of friends become family and lifelong bonds made. It was made more joyous by the occasion of Harriet and Geoffrey's wedding, the arrangements for which had been taken in hand by Lady Sylvia. Geoffrey had never realised just how much organisation went into a wedding!

Finally the day dawned.

The small village church was full, with the Hounds and their families, including Odette's aunt, Lady Farnsworth, plus Baron Setford, as well as all of the staff of both Pendholm Hall and Witherwood Chase, and most of the villagers and tenant farmers. Even Geoffrey's brother Alfred and his wife had deigned to attend. Geoffrey was darkly amused to discover that his new status as a man of wealth with substantial property appeared to have made him a more acceptable person in his brother's eyes.

As if any of those things mattered to him. Harriet was what mattered.

It was a day full of laughter and joy, with Harriet having chosen to wear a gown of spring green which set off her eyes, and Geoffrey looking elegant in simple black and white attire.

When the words had been said, and they walked from the church as man and wife, they were met with a cloud of rose petals to rival those that Geoffrey had arranged for Charlton's wedding. There was a very happy purveyor of hothouse flowers somewhere!

The only slight sad note in the day was Raphael's absence. It seemed that he had not yet returned from his latest travels. Geoffrey hoped that he might still arrive, before everyone departed in a week's time, as the Easter season ended.

They all returned to Witherwood Chase, to be served a sumptuous feast and dance in the newly renovated ballroom. Lady Sylvia had settled contentedly in a quiet corner, and was watching the festivities with great satisfaction.

Both of her children wed within a few months of each other, and both so happy – what more could a mother ask for?

At least Geoffrey and Harriet had not been forced to wait, as had Charlton and Odette, by the mourning period for Odette's father. She was not sure that Harriet's quicksilver temperament could have produced the patience to wait a year to wed!

She watched the people around her, noting who danced with whom (waltzes were so revealing of people's feelings...), and whose eyes followed who. There were some interesting possibilities before her – she wouldn't be at all surprised to see more weddings in the near future.

She was particularly delighted to see Lady Farnsworth dancing with Baron Setford. She rather thought that Lady Farnsworth's acerbic wit would appeal to Setford, and Lady Farnsworth deserved some companionship.

Also pleasing was seeing Miss Carpenter dancing with Mr Featherstonehaugh, who was cheerful and dapper as usual.

Miss Carpenter had been a patiently long suffering shadow to Harriet for so many years now that Lady Sylvia had been concerned for her future, once Harriet was wed. Perhaps there was nothing to worry about after all.

Setford's wedding gift to Harriet and Geoffrey had been a quietly delivered missive from the Prince Regent, which thanked them both for their recent actions to protect crown and country, and added a further grant of lands to Geoffrey's holdings.

He had confirmed that the remaining conspirators had been found and taken, that Jobs had been transported, and that the other two were held in Newgate, awaiting the hangman's pleasure.

The waltz ended, and Geoffrey swept Harriet out onto the terrace, where the sweet smell of the herbs in the scent garden drifted on the breeze as the Eastertide brought the growth of spring to the world. They stood, watching the stars, his arm holding her close to his side.

His voice was quiet, for her ears only.

"No more missions, no more searching. We can take life as we wish, go anywhere you wish. What do you wish, my darling Harriet?"

She stayed silent, thinking, at peace with the world. When, after some time, she spoke, it was a whisper, but her words were more powerful than a shout.

"It doesn't matter where we go, or what we do, so long as I can do it with you. Whatever may come, you will always be my hero."

The End

(You'll find a taste of book 5, "Enchanting the Duke" just after the 'About the Author' section in this book!)

AR
Arietta Richmond
Regency Historical Romance

About the Author

Arietta Richmond has been a compulsive reader and writer all her life. Whilst her reading has covered an enormous range of topics, history has always fascinated her, and historical novels been amongst her favourite reading.

She has written a wide range of work, from business articles and other non-fiction works (published under a pen name) but fiction has always been a major part of her life. Now, her Regency Historical Romance books are finally being released. The Derbyshire Set is comprised of 10 novels (7 released so far). The 'His Majesty's Hounds' series is comprised of 11 novels, with the fourth having just been released.

She also has a standalone longer novel shortly to be released, and two other series of novels in development.

She lives in Australia, and when not reading or writing, likes to travel, and to see in person the places where history happened.

Be the first to know about it when Arietta's next book is released!

Sign up to Arietta's newsletter at

http://www.ariettarichmond.com

When you do, you will receive a free copy of the <u>subscriber exclusive</u> novella **'A Gift of Love',** a prequel to the Derbyshire Set series, which ends on the day that 'The Earl's Unexpected Bride' begins

This story is not for sale anywhere – it is absolutely exclusive to newsletter subscribers!

Here is your preview of

Enchanting the Duke

His Majesty's Hounds – Book 5
Sweet and Clean Regency Romance

Arietta Richmond

Chapter One

The County of Berkshire, England – March 1814

The cold, spring air carried the last frosts of winter across the bleak countryside and nipped the exposed cheeks of the burly coach driver who steered the stately coach carefully through the wide wrought iron gates and into the grounds of Casterfield Grange. Frost-covered poplars lined the gravelled driveway and groundsmen in warm, long, woollen coats touched their hats in respect as the coach rolled by, wheels clattering on the small pebbles and steam swirling from the backs of the tired horses.

"Finally," whispered Lady Cordelia Branley, the elder daughter of the Baron whose family had held the noble title of Tillingford for nearly eight hundred years. She pushed her hands deeper into the fox-fur muff that kept her hands protected from the bitter cold and smiled.

"Home at last and we have arrived whilst it is still daylight."

Her companion (once her governess) tried to smile, but looked tired from the journey. Miss Millpost was a strict and severe spinster of some fifty summers, a woman whose main responsibility was to chaperone the pretty, dark haired sixteen-year old girl, teach her how to run a household as only a good and obedient wife should, and keep her out of mischief. The companion shifted her bony frame on the hard, leather-bound coach seat.

"How may we even know if the sun still exists beyond those dark clouds and the bitter cold? If I don't have warm tea to revive me, child, I fear I shall expire from the ague!"

Lady Cordelia tried not to laugh, for she knew that Miss Millpost would sooner revive her spirits with a glass or two of her father's excellent Madeira. She sighed. It felt good to be home once more, and she was more than excited to see her loving father again and her beautiful younger sister, Georgiana.

Ever since their dear mama had died, in a cholera epidemic when Georgiana was only five, Cordelia had tried to assume the role of mother, and she naturally felt deeply protective of her sister. The younger girl often behaved more like a boy and had seemed to prefer playing in the garden and getting herself covered in mud and leaves rather than learning to embroider and excel at the feminine arts. But their father loved them both dearly and indulged them in whatever ways might make them happy.

Despite the constant shadow of their mother's tragic death, it was still a happy household and a wonderful place to grow up.

Georgiana's insatiable curiosity had even prompted her father to consider appointing a tutor for his younger daughter and he was weighing the issue in his comfortable library with a pipe of fine Virginia tobacco and glass of good cognac when he heard the carriage wheels and the horses' hooves approaching the house.

Clouds of hot breath surrounded the horses as they pulled the carriage across the frozen ground and finally slowed to a welcome halt outside the grand entrance portico of Baron Tillingford's elegant home. Servants hurried to open the carriage door and unfold the steps so that the passengers could alight. They were smiling as Cordelia stepped down, obviously pleased to see her Ladyship safely returned from her journey. They fussed around her, almost ignoring the companion as she struggled to step down without lifting the hem of her heavy skirt and revealing her bony ankles. It was important to observe the correct proprieties at all times, she felt. Especially in front of the servants.

"Papa!" Cordelia cried as she caught sight of her father at the top of the steps. She raced up the broad stone stairs and hugged the Baron, who could barely contain his tears of joy as he held his lovely daughter in his arms and gave thanks for her safe return.

"You look so much like your beloved mama, my dear. How can I look upon you and not see the radiance of her grace and beauty? It warms my heart and cheers my soul!"

The companion coughed loudly behind Cordelia's back to announce her presence. "Miss Millpost. Well met and welcome back. You must join me in the library for a glass of light refreshment and tell me how went your visit to London."

Cordelia had not long celebrated her sixteenth birthday and the Baron had finally bowed to pressure from his precious elder daughter and allowed her to visit relatives in London. The Baron's cousin was influential and a well-known and popular guest in the salons and elegant drawing rooms of London's high society. The cousin and his wife would provide the perfect opportunity to introduce Cordelia to the nobility of the nation's capital.

At sixteen, the Baron was also aware that his daughter would soon be eligible for marriage and that it would do no harm for her pretty face and lovely smile to be seen in the discerning circles of the gentry. The hard fact was that the endless wars with Napoleon had taken far too many young men away from England's shores to offer their service in His Majesty's Army and Navy. And too few of them ever came back.

The result was that there simply were not so many young, eligible noblemen around who might come to Baron Tillingford and seek Cordelia's hand in marriage. Introducing the young woman into London society might possibly draw the attention of a noble young suitor, and then the ageing Baron could rest easier in the knowledge that at least one of his daughters had made a good match. It was all he wanted for his girls. To see them happily married and presiding over a great and noble household.

For, as he sadly had no son to follow him, the Barony, and its entailed estates, would pass to someone else, probably some extremely distant relative, or someone chosen by the King, as he had, to his knowledge, no male relatives to succeed him.

That made it all the more important that his girls be well placed with suitable husbands. He could leave them Casterfield Grange, for it was not entailed, nor were a few other properties he held, so their beloved home would still be theirs when he was no longer here to care for them. Still, he wished to see them happy, and married to men of suitable wealth and breeding, as soon as possible.

It wasn't too much to ask for, but the Baron was aware of his age and his growing infirmity. Time, he felt, was not on his side.

Chapter Two

London had been a revelation for the young Lady Cordelia Branley. She had danced until her feet hurt, charmed and excited by being so much in demand, and flushed with the attention of so many gentlemen. She had found many of those attentive gentlemen rather too old for her liking, and many were not so handsome of figure, no matter how elegantly dressed. Still their attention was flattering, and it was obvious that her beauty stood out amongst the girls present, with her striking dark hair and fresh skin. Many of the younger men seemed to avoid the dancing, perhaps because their families were pushing them to marry? Their absence initially disappointed her, but Cordelia soon discovered where they were hiding themselves during most of the Balls.

She'd been thrilled to see the well-dressed young bucks in their expensively-tailored attire, seated around card tables and wagering loudly on the outcome of every hand. Whilst the card rooms at Balls were more commonly frequented by men, and a few of the older ladies, only, Cordelia had begged her hostess for a chance to see what went on.

The games had been exciting to watch and, one evening, when one of the young nobles spied Cordelia and nodded his head at her with a courteous smile, it was all that she could do to contain herself. She blushed and the young man laughed, his carefully-oiled mass of dark curls set off with a black silk ribbon tied in a bow at the back.

He looked back at the table and roared with delight as he turned the final card and gathered up his winnings. His companions groaned as they threw their cards on the table and Cordelia turned to her hostess and asked who the young man might be.

"That is Lord Edward Fitzhugh, second son of the Earl of Bolton, my dear, a fine young man who should be alongside his father in the King's uniform, fighting the French in Spain. But he prefers to spend his days slug-a-bed and his nights gambling at the card tables and carousing."

Her hostess' voice was severe, quite disapproving, but she refused to say more on the matter. With her heart beating and her pretty eyes widening, Cordelia was utterly convinced that he was by far the most handsome young man she had seen.

Ever.

~~~~~

To one side of the room, an older gentleman, handsome, elegant and exquisitely presented, in attire that was in no way ostentatious, yet spoke, in its every line, of the best tailoring that money could buy, leant against the wall watching the room.
~~~~~

Philip Canterwood, Duke of Rotherhithe, enjoyed a hand of cards, but never gambled with any serious intent. He had just finished a game with some acquaintances, and now simply stood, quietly, watching. The behaviour of men when they gambled intrigued him.

The room was full of extravagantly dressed young fops, eager to display their wealth an unconcern for its loss, hoping, at every turn, to impress the young ladies who watched wide eyed. The fops might not yet wish to be captured into marriage, but they were hungry for a woman's admiration.

His gaze travelled around the room, alighting on a face he did not know. Beside Lady Mathilde Egremont stood a girl he had never seen before. She was young, and innocent inexperience showed in everything about her. But she was outstandingly beautiful, with rich dark hair, and glowing pale skin. Her lips, currently open in a small gasp, as one of the fops looked her way, were a delightful dark pink that fair begged to be kissed, if one were a man prone to kissing innocents.

Not usually one to be interested in the young girls, barely past childhood, that the mothers of the ton paraded in hopes of snaring a husband, he yet found himself watching this girl closely. Something about her drew him, as if, in some way, she might be different from the others.

He shook his head at his whimsy, and turned back to conversation with some friends, with a last faint wondering at who she might be.

~~~~~
~~~~~

During the following days, Cordelia conspired with her hostess to attend as many social functions as possible, overtly to meet as many noble ladies and gentlemen as she could but secretly with the hope that she might catch sight, once more, of the dashing Lord Edward Fitzhugh. Her hopes were not in vain.

Many of the great salons offered cards and the sport of wagering on the outcome, a pursuit that might have been reserved for the candlelit interiors of the gentlemen's clubs, but was widely accepted as a fashionable way to offer entertainment and draw the young bucks into the well-lit reception rooms where eligible young ladies might be viewed and appreciated for their potential as future brides.

Lord Edward was considered to be a most fortunate card player, for he displayed remarkable skill at the gaming tables. He always smiled and offered his fellow players a warm handshake when the games were done and he was filling his purse with his prize of gold coins.

On the final night of Cordelia's stay in London, she was sipping her glass of punch and watching the other guests in the elegant ballroom, when someone touched her bare shoulder and gently moved an artfully trailing curl of her lovely auburn hair aside.

She turned and stared into the pale grey eyes of Lord Edward Fitzhugh, and her heart nearly stopped beating.

He bowed to her, and when he looked up again he was smiling.

"Your servant, my Lady."

Miss Millpost, standing beside Cordelia, seemed on the verge of apoplexy when she noticed that the young Lord was being far too familiar with her charge, and without a formal introduction!

Cordelia, well used to Miss Millpost, was aware of her disapproval, and ignored it.

Miss Millpost would, no doubt, berate her soundly later. She was more interested in what Lord Edward had to say, than in Miss Millpost's opinion at that moment.

He looked into Cordelia's eyes and she found the intensity of his attention flattering, if almost unnerving.

"Pray, my Lady, would you grant me the boon of your favour and let me hear from your lips the sound of your name? For 'tis a perfect misery to my heart to behold your loveliness and not know how to address you."

At this rather overly dramatic pronouncement, Miss Millpost coughed so loudly that people in the vicinity turned to see if she were having a spasm, or a fit of the vapours.

"Sir!" she finally spoke with a steely edge to her voice. "You may address that question to me, for I am sure that you have not been formally introduced to the young lady and that you presume too much by speaking to her!"

The young lord laughed.

"The fault is entirely mine for forgetting my manners in the presence of such beauty. I was bewitched and enchanted by the lady's smile and I no longer know what I do."

Cordelia nearly clapped her hands in delight at his poetic manner, but managed to restrain herself beneath the watchful gaze of the disapproving Miss Millpost, who continued to speak to him firmly.

"Sirrah, I will have none of your poetry and nonsense! This is the elder daughter of the Baron Tillingford whose estates lie but two days' ride from London and whose family are well known to His Majesty the King! Who might you be, to presume so rudely to speak to her?"

Fitzhugh bowed deeply before Cordelia, with a dramatic sweep of his arm that brought his forefinger to almost touching the marble floor at the young Lady's feet, before drawing himself up to his full height and declaring, "And I am Lord Edward Fitzhugh, my Lady, and I am at your service."

Cordelia almost stuttered in the presence of the young Lord, so swept away by his looks and manner did she feel, but she made an attempt at appropriate behaviour, nonetheless.

"I am not at all certain, my Lord, that this represents a suitable introduction, to allow me to speak with you, within the bounds of propriety."

"Those foolish conventions apply only to the lesser mortals who strut but briefly upon this globe of dust and dreams. But you are divine, my Lady, a goddess, Venus herself come down from lofty Olympus to earth to torment the hearts of mere men and you have stolen both my wits and my heart, which I give to thee most gladly!"

Cordelia began to suspect that her heart would burst out of her chest as her face lit up with undisguised joy.

"I am Lady Cordelia, my Lord," she said, as she curtsied, "and I pray that I do not intrude too heavily upon your sensibilities."

"The intrusion is an oasis of perfect delight in this warren of the mediocre. Does a goddess require refreshment? More punch perhaps?"

Miss Millpost chose that moment to step purposefully between the couple.

"You have a way with words, Sirrah, and a pretty turn of phrase. Perhaps we should all go to the punch bowl to seek refreshment and ensure that the Lady's honour and reputation remain as pure and unsullied as they were when we first arrived."

With that, Miss Millpost took a firm grip on Cordelia's elbow and guided her in the direction of the long, white damasked refreshment table. She barely acknowledged the young Lord's presence, speaking only to Cordelia as they walked.

"It is insufferably warm in here and I believe a glass of punch would be most welcome to my poor dry throat."

Lord Edward took up station on the other side of Cordelia as the trio walked towards the crystal punch bowl. He waved away the servant with a brush of his hand.

"Dearest Lady, permit me."

He filled a glass with a small measure of the bright red liquid and offered it to Cordelia. As she took it in her lace-gloved hands, Edward filled a second glass to the brim and handed it to her companion.

"Your good health, Madame," he nodded at Miss Millpost as he raised his own glass in a simple toast, "and here's to your happiness and the loveliness of your eyes, Lady Cordelia."

He noticed how quickly Miss Millpost downed her punch, and quickly offered her a second.

"Thank you, Sir. I had not realised quite how thirsty one may become at these grand occasions."

By the time that Miss Millpost had consumed her third measure of punch, she was beginning to feel a little dizzy, and a little unsteady on her feet.

"Pray, child, but the heat is becoming too much for me and I fear I must sit." Cordelia helped her to an elegantly embroidered couch and eased her onto the seat where Miss Millpost promptly closed her eyes and fell soundly, but not noiselessly, asleep. Cordelia placed a cushion beneath her head for comfort and support, and the older lady began to snore softly. A small chuckle caught her attention. When she turned her head, she discovered that Lord Edward was standing behind her.

"My dear Lady. It would appear that the kind hand of Fate has cast us adrift without the restraining anchor of your companion." He smiled broadly at the young woman. "Perhaps you would care to accompany me for a while and enthral me with tales of life on your father's estate?"

They spent the next half hour standing in front of a wide fireplace, chatting to each other as the split logs crackled and the dancing flames lent their warmth and gaiety to the room. Lord Edward proved to be a most attentive listener and smiled at every nuance and detail that Cordelia shared with him.

For his part, he said very little, preferring to listen to the young heiress whilst cleverly eluding her questions with humour and evasive replies, implying that, despite his wealth and position, he really didn't take himself too seriously.

He seemed effortlessly charming, an open book, a man of wealth and position who only played cards for the fun of the sport, a man who enjoyed seeing his wealthy young friends squeal with horror whenever they lost. Which seemed to happen a lot.

A sudden and dramatic cough interrupted the young couple as Miss Millpost approached with a bleary eye and a slight waver in her gait.

"Ah! There you are, Lady Cordelia. I was resting my eyes for a moment and when I opened them again, you were gone."

Cordelia tried not to laugh.

"Yes, Miss Millpost, I saw that you were resting and I could not bring myself to disturb you. So I waited for you here by the warmth of the hearth and Lord Edward kindly volunteered to keep me company until you felt refreshed."

The companion cast a critical eye over Lord Edward and nodded her head.

"I see. Very thoughtful of the gentleman. Very thoughtful indeed. Well, we must be away. It is already late. I shall summon our carriage, for you will need your rest, if you are to be fresh for tomorrow's activities."

She turned on her heel and went to find a footman. Lord Edward murmured in Cordelia's ear, so close that she could feel the warmth of his breath upon her skin.

"She could probably outdrink half the men under service in His Majesty's Navy!" Cordelia laughed at his words, even as she felt a tingling warmth flow through her when the young Lord touched the tips of her fingers with his own. "And I would see you again, if you would permit me, sweet Lady Cordelia."

She smiled as she looked into his pale eyes.

"We leave for my home tomorrow morning, but I am sure that you would always be welcome to visit," she hesitated for a heartbeat, "for I would always be pleased to see you, Lord Edward."

Miss Millpost stepped back into the room and immediately seized the hand that she saw was far too close to the young Lord's fingertips. "Time to go, Lady Cordelia, time to go. Lord Edward, it was a pleasure meeting you. We shall take our leave and be on our way now."

"Farewell, Lord Edward," Cordelia spoke as she was half coaxed, half pulled from the room, "'til we meet again."

He bowed his head and blew a gentle kiss to her that she could've sworn had sailed across the widening gap that was opening between them and brushed against the smoothness of her beautiful cheek. She raised a gloved hand to her face in an attempt to hold the impression of the kiss upon her face for the rest of eternity.

Lady Cordelia Branley, Baron Tillingford's beautiful elder daughter, was hopelessly in love.

....

Read the rest as soon as it's released.......

Get

"*Enchanting the Duke*"

as soon as it's released – go to
http://www.ariettarichmond.com

and make sure that you are signed up for news and release notices !

Books in the 'His Majesty's Hounds' Series

Enchanting the Duke (coming soon)

Redeeming the Marquess (coming soon)

Healing Lord Barton (coming soon)

Winning the Merchant Earl (coming soon)

Loving the Bitter Baron (coming soon)

Rescuing the Countess (coming soon)

Attracting the Spymaster (coming soon)

Books in 'The Derbyshire Set'

Available at all good book stores and for ebook readers too!

Coming Soon!

Regency Collections
with Other Authors

Other Books from Dreamstone Publishing

Dreamstone publishes books in a wide variety of categories – here are some of our other bestselling books:-

We have books in many categories, ranging from Erotica and Romance to Kids Books, Books on Writing, Business Books, Photography, Cook Books, Diaries, Coloring books and much more. New books are released each month.

Be the first to know when our next books are coming out

Be first to get all the news – sign up for our newsletter at

http://www.dreamstonepublishing.com